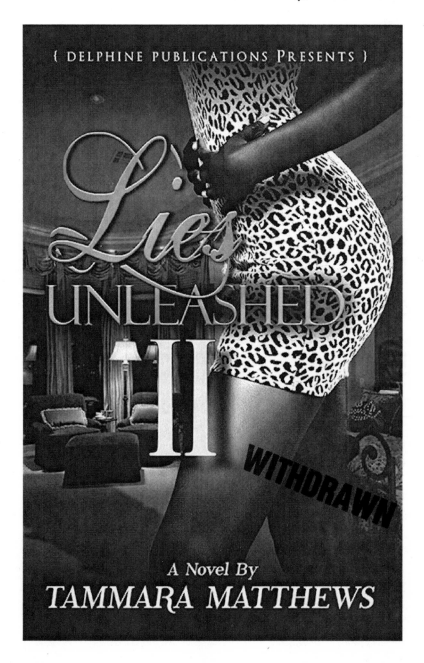

{ DELPHINE PUBLICATIONS Presents }

Lies
UNLEASHED
II

A Novel By
TAMMARA MATTHEWS

Lies Unleashed II

Delphine Publications focuses on bringing a reality check to the genre
Published by Delphine Publications

Delphine Publications focuses on bringing a reality check to the genre urban literature. All stories are a work of fiction from the authors and are not meant to depict, portray, or represent any particular person Names, characters, places, and incidents are either the product of the author's imagination or are used fictitiously, and any resemblances to an actual person living or dead are entirely coincidental

ISBN: 978-0989090636

Edited by: Tee Marshall
Layout: Write On Promotions
Cover Design: Odd Ball Designs

Printed in the United States of America

Dedication

Tamika Matthews who showed me that life is too short to waste time so take advantage of every moment and opportunity.

Lies Unleashed
II

Prologue

It's been six months since the trial, and everything's been peaceful up to this point. Candy found a new place to live on the other side of town, and Shawn was sentenced to seven years in prison for what he did, along with assaulting an officer. James hadn't been around since Shawn got locked up, but he still calls to check on me from time to time. Donte was never able to confront James about the letter he wrote to me, but he swears he got something for him the next time he sees him. So I'm just waiting around to see the drama unfold.

Chapter 1

Candy, Shawn, and Ariel

It's seven o'clock in the morning, and I'm heading upstate to see Shawn. I don't know how this is gonna play out, but I figured he needs to know he has a son. After getting processed and searched, I was told to sit at a glass window with a phone hooked to it. No sooner than I got comfortable, Shawn came out in an orange jumpsuit and sat on the opposite side of the glass.

"What you doing here?" he asked with a grimace on his face.

"I came here because we need to talk," Candy replied irritated.

"Talk about what? You did all your talking in the courtroom. As a matter of fact, don't come back here no more. We ain't got no words," Shawn said getting out of his seat to leave.

"Shawn, wait! You have a son!" Candy blurted out with a look of embarrassment on her face.

"I have a *what?*" Shawn said, slowly sitting back down.

"You have a son. I never lost the baby."

"And you're just now telling me this?" Shawn asked frustrated. "I told you from the beginning I didn't want no kids!"

"Well, you should've thought about that before you slept with me!" Candy yelled into the phone angrily.

"Bitch, you said you lost the kid, so don't try to pin no kid on me that ain't mine. I ain't got no kids!"

"You wanna bet?" Candy said staring him down. "Your little plan didn't work so I guess you paid all that money for nothing."

"I don't care what you say. That bastard ain't mine, so go find his real father."

"Alright, if you don't believe he's yours, then take a DNA test. If it proves that you're not his father, you'll never hear from me again," Candy said looking him in his eyes.

"Alright, when I gotta take it?"

"Next Monday."

"Fine," Shawn replied slamming the phone down and walking away. Now the only thing left to do is sit and wait.

Shawn

Two months have gone by since I found out Candy's baby is mine. I'm not thrilled about being a father, but it's nice to know I have a seed out there to carry on my name. Plus, after seeing a couple of pictures of the little dude, I had to admit he was pretty cute. He looks a lot like me too. After everything that's gone down, I've decided to get my life back on track seeing how I got a son and all. Today, I also found out that I'd be getting transferred to a new prison with less security, so things are starting to look up. On the bus ride to the new prison, all I could think about was my little man and how much of a fool I was, but all that's about to change.

After being searched and processed, a big burly white guard escorted me to my new cell. "Meet your new roommate, Big Rob. Have fun," the guard said sarcastically as he left me in there like a piece of meat facing a hungry lion.

"I knew I'd see your snake ass again. Now what was all that shit you was talking in court?" Big Rob said as he slowly stepped toward me while rubbing his hands together.

"Ain't nobody scared of your big ass. If you wanna do something, come with it," Shawn said ready to fight.

Ariel

I haven't heard from Mason in almost a year, and I'm still trying to find Nate's father. I've tested at least three dudes already and all of them tested negative. Who would of thought a night of lust and drinks would amount to this? What am I supposed to tell Nate? His mama was a ho? Ariel thought to herself as tears rolled down her cheeks.

After a long pause of silence she jumped off the couch and raced to the phone. "I think I know who it might be, or at least I'll keep my fingers crossed." Ariel quickly dialed the number, and a male voice answered the phone.

"Hey, are you able to talk right now?" Ariel asked hesitantly.

"Hold on," the man whispered into the phone. "Alright, it's cool now. What's up?"

"I have something important I need to tell you."

"Alright, I'm listening."

"You might need to take a DNA test because there's a

possibility that my son might be yours."

"What?" the man said as his heart sank down in his chest. "Are you sure about this?"

"Yes, I got pregnant around the same time we messed around, but I didn't want to call you until I was sure."

"How old is your son?"

"He's seven."

"And you waited *seven* years to do this?"

"No, my ex-husband found out he wasn't his father after having a DNA test done and left me. Now Nate doesn't have a father. I'm not trying to get you for child support or anything, I only want Nate to know who his father is."

After a brief silence and a deep breath the man spoke again. "Alright, man, when do you want me to take the test?"

"Are you available this Friday?"

"Yeah, I can do that."

"Thank you, I really appreciate it. Oh, and don't worry, your wife won't find out unless you want her to," Ariel said before hanging up the phone.

Candy

Today is my last day working at Club Fantasy and surprisingly Smitty didn't give me a hard time about leaving. My regular customers were a little disappointed when they found out, but for the most part, the day went smooth and the money flowed nice. Around time for me to leave, a few of the dancers even got together and threw me a going away party. All in all, I had a pretty nice day. After a whole lot of thought and convincing from Shawn, I finally decided to move to Miami, Florida. Shawn had been transferred to a penitentiary somewhere in Dade County so it had become too much of a hassle to make visitations. Besides, Shawn wanted to be closer to Shawn Jr. and I needed a change of scenery. Who would've thought Shawn would ever care about somebody other than himself? I sure didn't. Prison has changed him quite a bit though. He's no longer verbally abusive towards me and he doesn't cuss around Shawn Jr. He's even been on good behavior in hopes that they'll reduce his five-year sentence so he can spend more time with his son.

At first, I was kind of nervous about starting a new life. But now I'm looking forward to it. My cousin Tia offered me a place to stay until I get back on my feet and she even has a few jobs lined up for me. I'll still be stripping, but who knows I might finally get tired of it and decide to give it up, only time will tell. It's about six in the evening and I'm overwhelmed with boxes and packing, moving definitely ain't easy. My phone began to ring.

"Hello?"

"You have a collect call from, Shawn. Do you accept?" The audio voice sang through the phone.

"Yes."

"What's up? When you bringing SJ down for a visit? I miss my lil man?" Shawn asked me.

"I'm gonna try to bring him this weekend. I already got the plane tickets. I just gotta finish packing."

"Oh, that's cool."

"So what's going on with you? How are you holding up in there?"

"I'm cool; they got me sharing a cell with Big Rob. Can you believe that shit?"

"How did that happen, after he threatened to kill you?" I asked him concerned.

"I don't know man. All I know is he got one more time to get stupid with me and I'm a handle his ass. We already fought once, but the guards broke it up before it got to crazy."

"Why would they put y'all in a cell together knowing y'all history? That don't make no sense."

"Nothing ever makes sense around here. I just do what they tell me to do. Hopefully, they'll let me out on good behavior. I just gotta stay out of trouble." No sooner than Shawn could complete his last sentence, I began to hear sirens and people yelling in the background. "Shawn what's all that noise, are you alright?"

"Yeah, they putting the prison on lock down, somebody must've got stabbed or something."

"Oh my God! How can you be so calm?"

"Because this shit happens all the time. It used to bother me when I first got in here but now it doesn't phase me."

"I couldn't get used to that." I frowned

"Look, I gotta get off the phone. They're forcing everybody back to their cells. I'm gonna try to call you later, and tell SJ I love him."

"I will. Be careful Shawn." I heard one of the guards yelling for Shawn to get off the phone. Though he deserves everything he's getting, for the first time, I actually feel sorry for him.

A couple of hours later, after packing up most of my clothes, I heard a knock at my door.

"Who is it?" I yelled as I made my way to the door.

"It's me Niki."

"Hey." I smiled genuinely as we hugged.

"You need help packing?" Niki asked staring at all my boxes.

"I never thought you'd ask..."

"So have you heard from Shawn lately?"

"Yeah, a little while ago. Something was going on at the prison so he had to hurry up and get off the phone."

"Is he okay?" Niki asked me concerned.

"I hope so, he said somebody must've gotten stabbed or something, but he wasn't sure."

"Well I hope he's alright... So what are you gonna do once you move? Do you have any jobs lined up?"

"As a matter of fact, I do."

"Good, so what are you gonna be doing?"

"Well my cousin knows the owner of a really nice exclusive strip club in Miami so she's gonna hook me up with a job."

"So you're going back to stripping?" Niki looked at me confused.

"Pretty much, it's good money."

"I thought you wanted to quit?"

"I did, but ain't no job out here gonna pay me as much as I make stripping."

"Aren't you tired of doing that? I mean you have a son to worry about now and stripping isn't the safest job. There are some crazy men out here." Niki looked at me with disappointment on her face.

"Maybe so, but I need money."

"You can still make money with a regular job it's just not

fast money."

"That's exactly my point. I want my money when I want it and stripping gives me that option. Everybody's not meant to work a nine to five and besides, I like stripping."

"What is there to like about it? All day you have men gawking and trying to feel on you. Then to degrade you even more they throw one or two dollars at you like some cheap whore as if that makes everything okay." Niki replied unenthused.

"You know I'm sick and tired of people trying to preach to me about my job. The last time I checked I'm a grown woman so I can do whatever I want to do. I like stripping so I'm gonna keep doing it. Why can't y'all just respect that?"

"We can't respect it because it's a poor career choice and we know you can do better."

"Look, I don't want to talk about this anymore. I'm not gonna stop stripping so you might as well just drop it." I glared at Niki.

"Fine, it's your life you're ruining."

We sat in silence for a while until Niki spoke. "Well I gotta get ready to head out. I need to stop by the store." She stood and gathered her things. "Let me know if you need help with anything else. I'll have some free time tomorrow."

"Alright thanks for stopping by," I replied dryly. *I'm sick of people thinking they can tell me how to run my life. I can't wait to move away from here, at least then I'll have freedom to do what I want without having to hear people's opinions about it.*

Its six hours later and I'm still packing up boxes. I never thought I'd accumulated this much stuff. Tired, I decided to take a break and order some takeout. I heard a knock at the door as I picked up the phone to place my order. "Who is it?" I asked looking through the peephole.

"It's James."

"What do you want and how did you get my address?"

"Shawn gave it to me."

"He what!" Irritated, I snatched the door open. "Why are you here?"

"Look man this ain't the time for fifty thousand questions. Shawn's in the hospital and he asked me to tell you."

"What, is he okay?"

"He's been hurt pretty bad."

"What happened?"

"I don't know all the details. He only told me that he and Big Rob got into it. That's all he really had the strength to mumble out."

"How did he call you then?" I asked curious.

"The hospital called me and put me on the phone with him for a minute, but he couldn't talk long 'cause he was kind of in and out of it, plus I'm his emergency contact." James' words dripped with sarcasm causing me to roll my eyes.

"You can never just answer the question."

"Look, I didn't come here for all the drama. I'm getting ready to catch a plane out there to see him so if you wanna come along then be my guest, but if not I'll talk to you later." James headed for the door.

"How am I gonna get a plane ticket? They cost too much when you get them last minute." I complained.

"I got enough frequent flyer miles to get you one damn near free, just hurry up and get your stuff together if you coming."

James said as he sat on my couch in the living room.

"Hold on a minute let me call my Aunt and see if she can watch SJ until we get back."

"Where is he now?" James looked at me confused.

"He's with her so she probably wouldn't mind watching him."

After confirming that my Aunt would watch SJ for me, I rushed to get my things together. An hour later, we were heading out the door and on our way to the airport.

It didn't take long to get my ticket and board the plane once we arrived at the airport. Surprisingly, the security screening went pretty fast, which isn't often, so I was happy. "I'm surprised you're actually going to see him. He said he hadn't spoken to you since the day in the courtroom before he got shipped off to jail," I said to James while opening up a bag of complimentary peanuts.

"Yeah I know. I was kind of hesitant about going to see him, but I figured he's my brother and that's forever so I should at least go check on him."

"Yeah that's true. You think he's gonna be cool when he sees you seeing how y'all aren't cool like that?"

"He wouldn't have called me or listed me as his emergency contact if he didn't want to see me."

"Maybe you were a last resort." I stared at him.

"Are you gonna be talking the whole way there cause I really don't feel like hearing all that right now," James snapped at me. "As a matter of fact, do me a favor."

"What's that?" I asked confused.

"Be quiet." James turned his head towards the window and closed his eyes attempting to get some sleep.

"You are such an asshole." I glared at him.

"Thank you that's what I do best," he replied with a slight grin.

Once James and I arrived at the hospital I rushed to the counter. "Excuse me. We're looking for Shawn Davis. He was admitted sometime today."

"Just a minute ma'am." The nurse rudely replied as she continued to talk on the phone about her personal business. After five minutes of listening to who got whom pregnant, the nurse finally put whomever she was talking to on hold and placed the phone on the desk. "Now who are you looking for?" She asked with an attitude.

"I'm looking for Shawn…"

"Oh never mind, I got his chart right here." She said cutting me off. "Oh yeah, he's the one that got shipped here from prison." Her words echoed from the front desk.

"Well damn, thanks for letting everybody know. I'm sure all the patients are comfortable with everybody knowing their business." I sarcastically spat.

"Whatever, you can have a seat over there until you're called." The nurse rolled her eyes at me and went back to her phone conversation.

"I hate when they hire people like that. She don't have no type of customer service skills so how the hell did she get a job in customer service." I vented.

"Man didn't I tell you no talking." James said to me as he browsed through a sports magazine.

"Just because you let people talk to you any kind of way it doesn't mean I will."

11

"Yeah that's nice." James replied never looking up from his magazine.

"For real both of y'all can go to hell!" I moved two seats down from James wishing that he'd just disappear. A few minutes later, the rude nurse called us back to the front desk to meet the doctor caring for Shawn. "Are you two here for Shawn Davis?"

"Yes, I'm Candy and this is his brother James."

"Okay, I'm Dr. Larson, the one working with Shawn. He's doing much better than he was when he first came in, but he's gonna be here for a while until he's just about fully recovered."

"So is he able to have visitors?" James asked concerned.

"Yes he can have visitors, but he's been out since the surgery so he may still be asleep. We need him to take it easy. I'll take you to his room."

"Thanks Doctor," I said feeling more at ease.

"Excuse me," the rude nurse interjected. As James and I turned around the nurse handed James a stack of papers. "Oh and there's a little something in there for you." The nurse said winking at James while smacking on gum. As James flipped through the papers a small piece of paper, which had the nurses phone number and work hours written on it, fell to the floor.

"What's that?" I asked snatching the paper out of his hand. "I know that heffa didn't give you her number, she's got a lot of nerve. She didn't know if we were together or not!"

"She obviously didn't care either," James smiled.

"What's so funny? She totally disrespected me."

"You're getting all upset over nothing." James waved me off.

"I hate when females try to be slick." I rolled my eyes at

the nurse.

"Man stop tripping and come on. We're not here for that."

"I know. I just find it irritating that you dismiss it like its nothing."

"I'm not your man so why does it matter?"

"It's about respect," I attempted to explain.

"Will you just come on?" James walked ahead of me in hoping to shut me up. Little did he know he'd hear my mouth about it again later.

When James and I arrived at Shawn's room two cops stood patrol outside his door. "Who are you looking for?" One of the cops asked in an authoritative tone.

"I'm looking for Shawn Davis. His doctor told us this was his room. I'm his brother and this is the mother of his child."

"We need to see some identification before we can let you in his room." The other cop said sounding more genuine. Once we showed our ID's, the cops patted us down, followed us in the room, and stood guard by the door while we talked to Shawn.

"Hey," Shawn said sounding as if he'd just woke up.

"Hey, how are you feeling?" I asked concerned.

"I'm good, in a lot of pain, but the doctors been giving me medicine to ease it." He attempted to reach for the remote control.

"Let me get that for you," James said as he handed him the remote.

"I'm surprised you came to see me, Candy must've talked you into coming."

"No, actually I decided to come on my own and brought Candy along for the ride." James took a seat next to Shawn's bed.

"Oh? That's cool. I appreciate you coming to see me,

especially seeing how we ain't been getting along. I'm glad you here though." Shawn smiled avoiding eye contact.

"It's all good; you my brother regardless of everything that went down and family comes first especially when it involves you being in the hospital..." James looked at Shawn and shook his head. "So what the hell happened?

"Man I got caught in some bullshit. After I got off the phone with Candy, I got sent back to my cell and the prison was put on lockdown. Once everything got quiet the guards let us go to lunch, but when we got in the lunch room a fight broke out between two other dudes and while all the guards were trying to break up the fight, Big Rob bitch ass stabbed me."

"How did he get that close to you, you didn't see him?" James asked.

"Nah man, he wasn't even in the lunchroom at first so I don't know where he came from. Somehow, he snuck up behind me and jabbed me in the side with a shank. When I grabbed my side, that muthafucka stabbed me two more times in the chest and the stomach. The doctor was surprised the injury wasn't worse than what it was. He said I could've died."

"Damn." James looked at Shawn sympathetically.

"Anyway after that we went at it for a minute and somehow I managed to get the shank away from him and stab him in the chest."

"What happened after that?" I asked in shock.

"The guards came over and broke it up. I passed out after that so I don't know what happened beyond that point."

"Damn, is Big Rob still alive?" James asked.

"I don't know, but I hope not," Shawn said as he looked

down at his wounds.

"I'm glad you're ok," I smiled.

"Me too man, I got a son to think about now. I don't need all this crazy shit in my life. I'm trying to change, but it's hard to do in prison. People be testing you and I can't afford to be weak in there cuz that'll get you killed or somebody's bitch and that definitely ain't happening... Are y'all gonna be here for a while?"

"Yeah, if they let us we'll stay here overnight," James replied.

"It shouldn't be a problem as long as they know who y'all are. I'm gonna get some rest though cuz this medicine got me tired. Here's the remote control if y'all wanna watch some TV. I'll talk to y'all when I wake up."

"Well I guess we're gonna be here for a while. I'm gonna call my Aunt to check on Shawn Jr. I wanna see how he's doing." I darted over to the other side of the room to use my phone.

"That's cool. I'm a see what's on TV," James replied.

Chapter 2

Tanya

You put your all into one man and what do you get in return...nothing! I wasted so many years on this relationship when I could've been with someone who wants and appreciates me. I would give my life for this man if I needed to, but sorry to say I don't think he'd do the same. Yeah, he tells me he loves me and life wouldn't be the same without me, but does he really mean it? As soon as times get hard, he's ready to leave. Who knows, maybe he actually will one day. I'm constantly on pins and needles wondering if this will be the day that he actually leaves for good. I love him so much, but maybe that's the problem. I've become too dependent on him.

I was so much better when I was by myself. I didn't have these problems then. I didn't mind going to the movies or the mall by myself. If I wanted to do something, I'd get up and do it with no second thoughts. But now I don't anymore. I always want him to tag along. Mostly because if I don't he'll call me a million times or think I'm out with someone else. I hate love; it makes you silly and dependent. Well maybe not everybody, but with me it did.

Darnelle walked over towards me and asked, "Aye you ready to go?"

"Yeah just give me a minute," I said blowing out a breath of air.

"Well hurry up, I'm trying to get home before the game comes on. I don't wanna be out all night."

"You got it." I replied annoyed. We needed to go grocery shopping so I figured we'd go ahead and get it out of the way after I got off work. I didn't want Darnelle to come along but he insisted, saying that I'll spend all the money on nonsense if he didn't come with me. Like most women, I'm not always the fastest when it comes to shopping. And like most men, Darnelle is always in a hurry to get out. "Hurry up and get what you gonna get so we can go!" Darnelle fussed. I always have trouble deciding what I want for dinner and I get tired of making the same thing all the time. Sometimes I just want something different, but of course, he wouldn't understand seeing how he's not the one cooking. The only things he's concerned with is the TV program he's rushing back home to see and stuffing his face.

"Don't make this shit an all-night affair Tanya, let's go!" Darnelle yelled breaking my train of thought. At that point, I just hurried and grabbed what I could so we could go in order to shut him up. Once we got home, he went straight to the TV and I began to cook dinner. Every now and then, he would come in the kitchen to check on dinner.

"Damn baby what's taking so long, I'm hungry."

"I had to wash dishes."

"You ain't even started cooking yet? Man it's gonna be

about twelve o'clock before we eat!" Darnelle whined.

"It doesn't take that long to make spaghetti just give me a minute," I told him, irritated. Patience was a virtue Darnelle didn't have. If I flew off the handle every time he said or did something I didn't like I'd have one foot in the grave right now from heart attacks and stress. He finally left the kitchen and allowed me to finish cooking dinner. "Darnell will you help me put the food on the table?" It was about five-thirty when I finished cooking dinner and now here it is ten minutes to six and he's still not here to help. "Are you going to come help me or not?" I rolled my eyes annoyed.

"Yeah, here I come," he replied. After about ten minutes he finally comes strolling in to help after I've just about done it all myself.

"About time, it took you long enough," Darnelle said taking a seat at the table. I watched him as he scarfed down garlic bread and spaghetti like it was his last meal. When he finished he complimented my cooking and went back into the living room to watch TV. As usual, I cleaned the table and decided to take a nice hot bath to relax after a long day of working, cooking, shopping, and dealing with Darnelle.

As I entered the living room, Darnelle looked up and asked, "What you getting ready to do baby?"

"Take a bath."

"You want me to join you?"

"That'll be nice." I smiled feeling we could use some alone time.

"Alright, I'll be there in a few minutes." When I finished running my bath water, I got in the tub and waited for Darnelle to join me, but no shock to me, ten minutes later he still hadn't shown.

"Baby the water's ready are you coming?" After receiving no response, I went ahead and washed up and got out.

"You done already baby?" Darnelle asked barely looking up from the TV as I walked past him.

"Yeah, I got tired of waiting."

"Will you run me some water then?"

"Sure," I replied dryly through clenched teeth. After running his water, I went to bed and prepared to deal with the crap at work the next day.

Around two in the morning, I felt a hand sliding down my back. "Baby wake up." I heard Darnelle whisper into my ear.

"What..." I answered groggily.

"Baby turn over," he said as he kissed on my earlobes and neck.

"No I'm tired. I have to get up for work at six. Why did you wait so late?"

"It'll be quick I promise," Darnelle whined.

"Yeah right, you always say that," I said hoping he'd leave me alone.

"Come on baby I won't take long." Tired of hearing him grovel, I gave in.

"Fine, make it quick." I told him as I rolled over.

It's now almost an hour later and he's still going at it with no regard to the fact that I have to get up in a couple of hours. Now see, this is the reason why I didn't want to do anything! He never keeps his word. "Please tell me you're almost done," I said to Darnelle frustrated.

"Almost baby, just give me one more minute," he said as sweat dripped down his face and onto my chest.

"Baby please hurry up I need to go to sleep." No sooner than the words escaped my mouth, Darnelle began to jerk and let out a loud grunt. "Damn that was good baby I needed that." Then he turned over to go to sleep. He could've at least held me or something. I stared at him as anger rose from my chest. Now look at him, he lies there sleeping like a baby while I'm stuck looking up at the ceiling and counting sheep. *Inconsiderate bastard. I should wake his ass up.* I thought to myself then decided against it.

Around six in the morning I got up and headed into work feeling tired as hell. I got bags all under my eyes and I seriously don't feel like being bothered but that's damn near impossible. I don't usually get up this early for work, but it takes me a minute to get there in rush hour traffic and my boss is meeting with a client today so the conference room has to be set up. After I finished setting up the conference room and brewing coffee Shelly, the other secretary my boss recently hired, walked in. "Hey Tanya I'm gonna go out and grab a bite to eat."

"Didn't you just get here?" I asked her irritated.

"Yeah, but you know how I am without my morning coffee," Shelly said then headed out the door.

After a minute or so, she peeked her head back in the door and asked, "Oh, will you pick up my calls for me?"

"I have…"

"Thanks Hun," she replied and was out of the door again before I could even respond.

I swear that girl gets on my last nerve. She has to be the laziest white girl I've ever met and she's always trying to throw her work off on everybody

20

else, mainly me. Mr. Conway only hired her because of the way she looks. Blonde hair, blue eyes, and long legs get you a long way at this job. She spends practically her whole day on break. "Tanya have you seen Shelly?" My boss, Mr. Conway asked snapping me out of my trance.

"She stepped out for a moment."

"Okay, will you tell her to stop by my office when she gets back?"

"Yes sir, will do."

My phone rang as I sat at my desk filing papers. "Did you call the electric company like I asked you to do?" Darnelle spat through the phone.

"No not yet, I've been pretty busy at work so I haven't had a chance to."

"Why didn't you call them before you left this morning?"

"They weren't open yet." I spat with attitude.

"You need to call them whenever you go on break. We just got a late notice in the mail for the bill."

"I'll try to as soon as I get a break," I replied irritated.

"I don't need you to try I need you to actually do it." Darnelle spat through the receiver. "Why can't you do it? You're off work today?"

"The bill's in your name that's why." Darnelle yelled. "They know who you are Darnelle, you've called them before. That's why I had them put you on the account."

"Look, take care of the bill," Darnelle sternly repeated into the phone and hung up.

As usual, everything is left on me! You'd think I was superwoman with all the crap I have to do. I swear I should take a vacation and not tell anybody where I'm going.

21

Thirty minutes later Shelly came walking through the door with coffee in one hand and shoes in the other. "Went shoe shopping huh?" I asked as she sat down at her desk.

"Yeah, I saw these on sale, so I figured I'd grab them. Did I have any calls?"

"Mr. Conway needs to see you." I replied ignoring her question.

"Okay, thanks Hun." Shelly said as she sauntered to Mr. Conway's office.

It's one o'clock and I still haven't had my lunch break. What the hell is taking her so long? I headed to Conway's office and was stunned by what I saw when I walked in. All I could do was stand there with my mouth hanging open as I watched Conway plunge his manhood into Shelly while she bent over his desk. "Oh my God." Was the only thing I managed to get out of my mouth as I watched him hold on to her hair for leverage with each thrust.

"Ms. Whitfield!" Mr. Conway yelled as I ran out of the office. About ten minutes later Mr. Conway came storming over to my desk. "Why didn't you knock first?"

"Why were you having sex with your secretary in your office? The last time I checked I thought you had an open door policy. I guess I know what you mean now. And no wonder she gets treated so much better than I do you're screwing her."

"And how do you figure that?" Conway asked with a confused look on his face.

"Let's see, she hasn't even been here six months yet and she's already gotten a raise. She came in with hardly any experience compared to my ten years, but she makes more than I do. She takes off whenever she wants and is never reprimanded while I've only taken off maybe three times since I've been here and I received a letter of counseling. She never does her work so I am forever picking up her slack. She comes and goes whenever she feels like it during work hours. I guess you thought I was stupid and wouldn't notice the perks you've been giving her. Oh and I didn't know shoe shopping was one of our job duties." I sarcastically stated.

"What is this talk about shoe shopping and…"

"Here you go," I interjected, holding the shopping bag in front of his face.

"What is this?" Mr. Conway asked snatching the bag out of my hand.

"Shelly's new boots she bought during work hours."

"Maybe she was on break." Conway said smugly.

"According to this time card she wasn't and I know I didn't break her considering she had just got here."

"You had no business…

"What, expecting fair treatment?" I interjected. "I'm sure the Better Business Bureau along with your wife would love to hear what you do with your employees. It's all part of the job right?" I glared at him as his pale face turned slightly red. "You know I've had enough excitement for one day so I'll be back tomorrow. That way you'll have time to figure out how you want to handle this situation." With that said, I grabbed my things and headed out the door.

"What the hell are we gonna do now?" Mr. Conway said as he stormed into his office.

"What do you mean?" Shelly asked confused.

"What do I mean? Tanya caught us having sex. I have a wife and kids at home to worry about and she knows all of them."

"So, what's your point?" Shelly asked as she stared him down.

"My point is I may be in some serious shit."

"If you're getting a divorce why would it matter if your wife found out?"

"Because she can take me for everything I have. I'll be damned if I end up homeless and poor because of you." Mr. Conway nervously paced around the office.

"Excuse me, what the hell is that supposed to mean?" Shelly asked with her hands planted on her hips.

"You're not worth me losing my family over."

"You lying bastard, you said you were getting a divorce!" Shelly exclaimed.

"And you actually believed it. I have kids to think about!"

"You weren't thinking about your wife and kids when you were fucking my brains out. But now all of sudden they're so important! You're so full of shit, you think you have a problem on your hands with Tanya knowing well wait to you get a load of me!" Shelly said as she stormed out the office. "Damn what have I done?" Conway mumbled to himself as he buried his face in his hands.

"Baby you would never believe what happened at work today," I said to Darnelle as I walked through the door.

"Did you take care of the electric bill?" Darnelle rudely interrupted.

"Yeah."

"Good, now what did you wanna tell me?" Darnelle asked as he stared at the TV.

"Nothing, I'm good," I replied dryly.

"So what are we having for dinner tonight?"

"I'm not sure what do you want?" I asked pissed at Darnelle's lack of consideration.

"Make whatever, you know what I eat." With that said, I headed to the bedroom to get more comfortable. I laid across my king sized bed and began to think about the events of the day. My thoughts were interrupted by Darnelle yelling, "Baby at four o'clock you have to go pick Danielle up from your mother's house!"

"Why can't you pick her up? It's not like you're doing anything! I can't do that and cook dinner at the same time I'm not Superwoman Darnelle!"

"It's my day off so I'm relaxing," Darnelle spat with attitude.

"Well I just got off work and I think I deserve a break too. I work just as hard as you do!"

"Yeah I hear you, but like I said she has to be picked up by four o'clock."

"You know what? I'm sick of this shit! I have to do damn near everything while you sit your lazy ass around the house and do nothing. Last time I checked we were in a relationship where both of us are supposed to share the responsibility."

"I'm not gonna sit here and argue with you Tanya just do like I asked!"

"Don't talk down to me! I'm not your child!"

"Tanya you need to lower your voice. You're still gonna have to pick her up so there's no point of continuing this argument." Darnelle said in a condescending tone.

"You know what? It's fine. I'll pick her up. Just don't be

expecting dinner tonight."

"What you mean? You should've already started on that." He stood in the doorway of the bedroom with a confused look on his face.

"Darnelle I haven't had time to cook dinner. I just got in the house from work."

"Well do it when you get back."

"That's not happening Darnelle. I suggest you order out."

"I'm sure you can manage to cook something. Just do it when you get back like I said."

"I'm done Darnelle. Say what you want but it's not happening." I said then headed for the door.

Three hours had passed and I still hadn't made it home with Danielle. He had been calling my phone repeatedly, but I just let it go straight to voicemail every time.

I know damn well she should've been home by now. It doesn't take that long to pick Danielle up from her grandmother's house especially seeing how she's only fifteen minutes away. No sooner than he thought the words, Danielle and I came walking through the door. "Daddy," Danielle yelled as she ran into his arms.

"Hey baby," Darnelle said as he leaned over and kissed her on the cheek.

"How was school baby?"

"It was good. We had a lot of work to do, but I finished all mine at Grandma's house." Danielle said with a smile as she picked her book bag up off the floor.

"Good baby, now go ahead to your room and change clothes. I don't want you getting your school clothes dirty." After sending Danielle to her room, he stormed over to me and tightly grabbed my arm. "Where the hell have you been?" He asked as he shook me.

"Let me go Darnelle!"

"Not until you tell me where you've been with my daughter!"

"I'm not telling you anything until you let go of my arm!"

"Tell me where you've been!" Darnelle yelled losing patience.

"Let me go!" I yelled in pain as Darnelle tightened his grip on my arm and jerked me towards him.

"We went and grabbed something to eat!" I responded as I tried to loosen his grip.

"Bullshit!"

"Let me go!"

He grabbed me by my throat and pinned me against the wall. "Look you do whatever the fuck I tell you to do!"

"Please let me go!" I gasped as tears welled up in my eyes.

"I shouldn't have to tell you shit twice. Now let me have to say it again and next time I won't be so nice! I can show you better than I can tell you!" He shoved me into the wall by my throat and said, "You ain't moving fast enough, I don't smell nothing cooking!" When he finally released his hold, I slid to the floor. I couldn't believe what had just happened. After a few minutes passed, I slowly eased up off the floor and made my way to the kitchen. I seriously contemplated putting bleach in his soup, but later decided against it figuring it would be too obvious and all the evidence would point to me. *As God is my witness I'm gonna get him back.*

Later that night, I lay still on my side of the bed and

attempted to go to sleep as tears rolled down my cheeks. *What have I gotten myself into?* As I wiped away my tears, I heard Darnelle whispering my name as he made his way over to the bed.

"Tanya…." I didn't respond.

"I know you're awake." He said noticing that my eyes were open.

"What do you want?"

"Baby I'm sorry for what I did to you. When I noticed you weren't home, yet I was pissed. I hate not knowing where you are. It worries me, especially since you had Danielle. These streets ain't safe out here, anything could've happened to y'all and I wouldn't have known a damn thing. So when you didn't answer your phone I flipped out… Though I felt the way I felt, there's no excuse for me putting my hands on you so I am truly sorry for that and would like you to forgive me eventually." He placed a dozen roses next to me and caressed my back, but I jerked away. "I'll let you get some rest." Then he left the room. Staring at the roses, I sniffed them slightly then pushed them to the side. *Roses and candy used to work for me when things like this happened, but this time I don't think it's enough. Something's gotta give or else I'm filing for divorce.*

Chapter 3

Ariel

After a lot of tiptoeing around and rescheduling, I was finally able to get the DNA test done to find out Nate's real father, who is a man name Keith Dawson. When I received the results I called him hoping he'd to want to be a part of Nate's life but the moment he found out he started playing me to the left, claiming that he needs to get his family used to the idea of him having another child. Can you believe that shit? I sure as hell couldn't! Anyway I remember when I first met Keith, I thought he was funny, exciting, and easy to talk to. Just being around him made me forget I was married, but that was before I lost my husband. Bare with me as I explain how my affair with Keith began and left me where I am today, bitter and alone. I met Keith Dawson at a lounge a few years after me and Mason got married. Me and my girls decided to have a girl's night out since we hadn't done it in a while. We went to this new lounge that had opened up a while back called the Escalaver, which ended up being pretty nice. My intention wasn't to go looking for men, he just happened to capture my attention. I was sitting at the bar drinking a Long Island Iced Tea when he approached me. He had this boyish charm about him that kind of lured me in. He was about 6'2" with dark brown eyes, a close cut fade, and skin the color of nutmeg. The fact that he had the body of a God and he was extremely handsome didn't help either. He cracked a smile and showed me the whitest teeth I'd ever seen and asked me if I'd dance with him. Of course, me being me I had to take him up on his offer.

As we slow danced things started to get a little hot and heavy. I began grinding on him and he softly kissed me on my neck. I then felt his hand slide around my waist as he guided my hips. "Ummm." I heard him mumble in my ear. He slowly turned me around and gently kissed me on my lips. "Tastes good," he whispered in my ear. "You wanna get out of here?"

"I don't think that's a good idea."

"You'll be safe with me I won't hurt you," he whispered.

"I came here with my friends."

"I'll drop you off at home. We don't have to go back to my house or anything. We can go get something to eat. I just wanna know more about you." Keith smiled.

"I don't know. I barely know you."

"I promise we'll only get food and I'll drop you off at home."

"Okay, I guess, but if you try anything funny I got the cops on speed dial," I warned.

While riding to get something to eat my cell phone rang. "Where are you?" The male voice spat through the receiver.

"I'm out with my girls. I told you earlier we were going out tonight."

"Ariel it's three o'clock in the morning, you should be at home! Do you know how long I sat here waiting for you? We had plans to go out!"

"I had some things to do," I nonchalantly stated.

"That's bullshit Ariel! You've been gone since twelve o'clock this afternoon. Did you forget we had dinner reservations? It's our anniversary. Is going out with your girls more important than that?" Mason said. I could hear the disappointment in his voice. "I can't believe you. You're so childish and irresponsible!"

"Look I have to go can we talk about this later?" Ariel rudely spat into the phone.

"Are you serious, you have to go where?"

"Alright I'll talk to you later," I said and hung up in Mason's ear.

"That's your man?" Keith asked with a slight smile.

"Something like that." I smiled back.

Keith took me to a place called My Little Tavern. And no sooner than we arrived Mason was blowing up my phone again.

"Look I'll call you later, I'm busy!" I hung up in Mason's ear.

"Do we need to postpone this get together?" Keith asked with his eyebrows raised.

"No we're good."

"What can I get you two tonight?" A young female waitress asked with her pen and pad in hand.

I asked, "Do you all have Long Island Iced Tea?"

"Yes ma'am we do," The waitress smiled.

"Okay, I'll have one of those."

"Sure, and for you sir?" The waitress asked looking at

Keith.

"I'll have a rum and coke."

"Alright I'll be right back with your drinks." The waitress smiled then walked away.

After three Long Island Iced Teas, not including the drinks I had earlier, I was done. As Keith asked me questions about my job and home life, I did the best I could to answer through slurred speech.

"You ready to go?" Keith asked noticing I was a bit drunk.

"Sure." As I slowly stumbled towards the car, Keith guided me in the right direction.

"Where would you like me to drop you off?" Keith looked seductively in my eyes.

"I'm not ready to go home yet. Can we chill at your place for a while?"

Keith looked at me with concern. "Are you sure about that? I don't want no Ike and Tina situation occurring on account of me. Your dude seemed a little upset about you being out this late."

"I'm not worried about him. He's not the boss of me."

"Alright then we can go to my spot," Keith replied hesitantly. A little while later, we pulled up to a big, beautiful red and white brick house with a three-car garage. As we walked inside, I was stunned to see how immaculate and nicely decorated the house was.

"Is this your house?"

"Yes, it's mine."

"Do you stay here by yourself?"

"Of course I do," Keith smiled slightly.

"What do you do?"

"I'm an investor. I help people manage and invest their money."

"It sure must pay well," I smiled.

"Do you want anything to drink?" Keith gestured for me to have a seat.

"No thanks. I think I've drunk enough. So what is a handsome man like you doing in this big ole house by yourself?" I asked as I made myself comfortable on the living room couch.

"Me and my ex broke up about a year ago so I've been staying here by myself ever since."

"Oh, sorry to hear that." I gazed at him.

"So what's the deal with you and your dude?"

"We're not doing well right now. We're always arguing and I'm tired of him always trying to keep tabs on me. I can never go out and have a good time without him blowing up my phone. I just want to chill out with my girls without having to deal with all that."

"Yeah I can understand that." Keith agreed while sipping on a glass of Rum and Coke.

"Can I have a sip?" I asked wondering what he was drinking.

"Um yeah." Keith passed me his glass.

"Ummm…Rum and Coke man huh?" I smiled as I passed his glass back to him.

"Yeah that's me, you want something?"

"I don't know I really shouldn't drink anymore tonight."

"Its just one glass I'm sure it won't hurt. Besides, I don't like drinking by myself it's always better with company." Keith smiled at me. I thought about it for a minute and figured why not.

It felt kinda awkward watching him drink while I drank nothing.

"Ok Sure, what you got?"

"Let me surprise you." He headed towards the kitchen and a few minutes later, he came back with a Mudslide with crushed ice in one hand and an Absolut and cranberry in the other.

"I'm already drunk. You're really trying to get me messed up." I took a sip of my Mudslide. "This is really good what did you put in it?"

"That's for me to know and you to never find out," Keith teased.

"When I was in college I used to bartend to make extra money and let's just say I add a little bit extra in my drinks."

"Extra like what?" I glared at him.

"Not extra like date rape drug extra." Keith stared back with a look of insult. "Don't worry. Drugging women and bringing them back to my house is not my thing. Every woman I've ever been with did it on her own free will."

"That's good to know." I exhaled relieved. After a few more drinks and a lot of flirting, Keith turned on some music and guided me to the middle of the floor. "Are you too drunk to dance with me?" He asked pulling me close to him.

"No I'm good."

As we slow danced things began to get heated and from behind, Keith nibbled and kissed on my neck. "You like that?" Keith slowly turned me towards him.

"Yes," I whispered. Keith gently grabbed my chin and kissed me softly on the lips. Unable to resist, I kissed him back. With even more passion than before Keith pulled me into him and held me tighter as we kissed. He began to unbutton my blouse while planting slow kisses down my neck and back. "Umm…"I moaned. Drunk and horny, we stumbled over to the couch to finish what we started, nothing else needed to be said.

The next morning I opened my eyes as the sun beamed in my face. I sat up slowly and noticed nothing looked familiar to me. *Oh my God what have I done?* I looked at the clock next to the television. *It's 9:30 in the morning! Oh no what am I gonna do? How am I gonna get out of this one? I wasn't supposed to stay this long.* I quickly hopped off the couch and headed towards the bathroom. Locking the door behind me, I frantically checked my cell phone messages. "You have 16 new messages," the voicemail sang through the phone.

"Where the hell are you? It's four o'clock in the morning?" Mason yelled through the phone. I immediately erased the calls not wanting to hear the rest of the messages he had left. I crept out the bathroom and tiptoed past Keith. I grabbed my things and headed out of the front door only to realize that I didn't have my car. *Oh shit, I didn't drive!* I stood outside the front door feeling like an idiot.

"You alright Shorty?" Keith asked as he stood behind me in the doorway stretching.

"I forgot I didn't drive last night."

"It's okay I'll take you home." Keith grabbed his keys.

"That might not be a good idea."

"What you don't trust me? If I didn't hurt you all this time I'm not gonna," Keith said sounding confused.

"No it's not that, my husband might be at the house."

"Okay so what do you want to do?" Keith replied.

"Give me a minute I'm gonna call my friend Dana. Maybe I can get dropped off at her house." The phone rang four times before Dana picked up.

"Hello?"" Dana yawned. "Hey it's Ariel."

"Girl what happened to you last night? The last time we saw you, you were dancing with that dude?" Dana asked concerned.

"Don't worry I'm alright. I'll explain everything to you later. Anyway, can I come over to your house?"

"When?" Dana asked me confused.

"Right now, Keith's gonna drop me off."

"Who is Keith?" Dana sat up in her bed.

"Look I'll explain all that to you when I get there, can I come over?"

"Yeah I'll be here."

"Alright thanks girl." I gave a sigh of relief.

"No problem." Dana said as she hung up the phone.

"So what's the plan?" Keith asked breaking the silence.

"I'm gonna get dropped off over my friend Dana's house."

"Alright then let's head out."

Once I arrived at Dana's house, I explained my situation hoping that she would agree to help me with the story I'd concocted on the way over. "So will you say I was here last night?"

"Fine I'll do it." Dana was disappointed but she agreed.

"What's wrong?" I asked noticing the look on Dana's face.

"You know you wrong right? You have a good man at home that will do just about anything to make you happy and you treat him like crap. I would love to be in your shoes and have a man to treat me the way Mason treats you. He married you despite all your flaws and issues and yet you spent your anniversary with another man when you should've been with him."

"Look Dana, spare me the lectures. I really don't feel like hearing all that right now." I sighed irritated.

"Alright I'll leave you alone, just know it's only but so much that man's gonna take before someone else comes along and do what you wouldn't do." Dana said holding her hands up in surrender.

"And what is that exactly?" I stared her down. Dana turned around, looked at me and shook her head. "Love him and treat him the way he deserves to be treated."

"If I didn't know any better I'd think you want Mason for yourself."

"No sweetheart. I don't want him I can get my own man, but that doesn't mean another woman won't. You better step your game up or you won't have him for long." Dana said as she headed into the next room. *Whatever she can't tell me nothing. She don't even have a man.*

Content with my lie I finally decided to give Mason a call back. "Hello," Mason answered.

"Hey baby it's me."

"Yeah I can see that." Mason replied obviously irritated.

"I'm sorry about last night. I had a little too much to drink so I crashed over Dana's house for the night."

"Yeah I hear you." Mason responded, I could tell by the tone in his voice that he didn't believe a word I said. "When are you coming home?"

"I'll be there in a little bit."

"What is a little bit an hour, two hours, what?" I could hear the anger in his voice.

"Give me about an hour."

"Alright." He said then abruptly hung up the phone. *Looks like I got some making up to do.*

Chapter 4

Charlene

After everything we've been through me and Mason are still going strong. Mason's career has taken off into a new direction and everything is better than ever. Sometimes Ariel still attempts to call him claiming that the DNA test may have been wrong, but he's not going for it. He refused to take another test and even changed his number so she couldn't contact him anymore. I, on the other hand, am a different story. Lately I haven't been feeling that well. I can't seem to keep anything down and I'm tired all the time. Considering this, I have a doctor's appointment today and I'm not too thrilled about it because I'm afraid to hear the outcome. As I sat on the couch deep in thought, I heard my doorbell ring. I smiled at Niki when I opened the door, happy that she was able to come to the doctor with me on such short notice.

"Hey girl you ready to go?" Niki asked as she walked through the door.

"Yeah I'm ready. Let me get my coat."

"Are you all right?" She asked as we headed to the car.

"No, I'm scared Niki. If I'm pregnant what am I gonna do? I don't know how to take care of no kid. I've never been pregnant before… maybe I should have an abortion if I am."

"Charlene you don't even know if you're pregnant yet and if you are maybe you should talk to Mason before you make a decision like that."

"After Ariel, Mason said he doesn't want any kids. He seemed pretty adamant about not having any." I looked out the window.

"Once he hears that you're pregnant he might change his mind. Weren't you on birth control?"

"Yeah that's what I don't understand Niki. I took those damn pills faithfully so I don't know how this happened."

"Everything's gonna be okay Char. Just stop worrying. We'll see what the doctor says." As I sat in the doctor's office anticipating the results I began to think of how good a father Mason would be. *Only if he wanted kids.* "We have your results." The doctor said breaking my train of thought. "It looks like you're pregnant and the ultrasound showed you're having twins."

"Oh my God!" I broke down into tears. "What am I gonna do, he doesn't even want one kid let alone two. I can't have these kids Niki. I will not be a single mother." I sobbed.

"Mason is not gonna leave you just because you're pregnant. You should know him better than that. Just tell him what's going on, it's not like you can hide it from him he's gonna find out eventually."

"I know." I wiped tears from my eyes.

"It's gonna be okay Char. Don't worry, just talk to him," Niki reassured me.

Wiping my face with a napkin, I agreed and began thinking of ways to break the news to Mason.

I was lost in thought as I walked in the house with tears streaming down my face. Exhausted, I kicked off my shoes, curled up on the couch, and dozed off to sleep. Two hours later, I was awakened by a soft kiss on my forehead. "Hey baby." Mason said with a smile on his face. "Are you hungry, I brought you something to eat?"

"Thank you baby, but I'm not really hungry."

"Baby what's wrong?"

"Nothing, I'm just not feeling to well."

"Do you need to go to the doctor?" Mason asked me worried.

"No, I went earlier today."

"So what did they say?"

"I really don't want to talk about it." Tears began to roll down my cheeks.

"Baby what's going on? Was it that bad?" I slowly pulled myself up to a seated position. "I have something to tell you, you might want to sit down." Mason examined the look on my face, and then slowly sat down. "Okay what's up?" A nervous feeling arose in the pit of Mason's stomach as he impatiently waited to hear my next words. "I'm pregnant."

"You're what?" Mason stared me down.

"I'm pregnant, I found out today when I went to the doctor."

"You're pregnant?"

"Yes Mason." To my surprise, he slowly cracked a smile.

"We're gonna have a baby?"

41

"No actually two."

"Two what?" Mason looked at me confused.

"Two babies, I'm pregnant with twins."

"Yeah!" Mason yelled leaping off the couch. Surprised by his reaction I stared at him. "You're not mad?"

"Mad for what?"

"About me being pregnant?"

"Why would I be mad? I think it's great!" Mason smiled.

"Okay, now I'm confused. I was under the impression that you didn't want any kids after dealing with Ariel."

"I wanted kids, just not with the wrong person. I didn't want to end up in the same situation I was in with Ariel." Mason clarified.

"Well it looks like you're gonna be a daddy!" I smiled feeling more at ease.

"Get dressed baby we're going out to celebrate." Mason kissed me on the lips and rushed off to get dressed.

As I got dressed, I gave Niki a call.

"So what happened?" She asked after picking up on the first ring. "Did he flip out, am I gonna have to come over there?"

"No everything's good, he's actually really happy about it."

"Okay then why do you sound so down?" Niki asked concerned.

"I'm scared with this being my first baby and all. I don't know how to take care of no kids Niki, and just to think I'm having two."

"Charlene when you see those babies you'll know what to do and if you don't, you have people around you who are happy to help. You have a good man who wants to be there for you and the babies, happy grandparents, and a friend who will always be here for you when you need me. Believe me, the way you and Mason are your kids are gonna be spoiled as hell." Niki laughed.

"Yeah I guess you're right, I'm just trying to take it all in."

"So what are you getting ready to do?" Niki asked.

"Mason's taking me out to dinner to celebrate."

"Oh that's nice, I'm gonna let you finish getting ready then. Tell Mason I said congratulations and do me a favor, stop worrying. Everything's gonna be just fine. I'll talk to you later."

"Baby you okay?" Mason asked as he walked into the room.

"Yeah, I'm just nervous about the babies."

"There's no need to be nervous baby, I'll be here for you through the whole thing. Everything's gonna be fine I promise." Mason said with a smile as he hugged me tight. "Now call Niki back. Her and Donte are coming with us to celebrate. I talked to Donte when he was leaving work so he should be heading home to get changed now."

"Umm I like a man who takes charge," I smiled slyly.

He gave me a kiss on the lips and said, "Do you really now? Wait until the babies come, you're really gonna love me then."

Chapter 5

Shawnn

It's seven o'clock in the morning and I'm just waking up. "What are y'all doing here?" I asked attempting to sit up in bed.

"The hospital called us remember?" James replied.

"How long have I been out?"

"Since your surgery yesterday, about 12 hours."

"Damn that long?"

"Yep that long." James replied. "So did you ever find out what happened to Big Rob?"

"Yeah, I overheard a couple of the nurses talking about how they were surprised he made it in the condition he was in. I guess I got him pretty good." I adjusted my cover. "I'm glad he didn't die though, the last thing I need is a murder charge on my record. They probably would've tried to give me life over that shit and I didn't even start it."

"So when are they sending you back to prison?" Candy asked.

"Supposedly in a couple of days, are you still moving out here?"

"Yeah, I'm almost done packing so by the time they send you back I should be heading out this way," Candy replied.

"Cool, I like the fact that I'll be closer to my son. I don't want him to end up like me though…" I looked at James. "James, I know you don't really deal with me like that and after everything I did to you I don't blame you, but I want you to know that I appreciate you coming to see me and bringing Candy with you. I did you dirty, especially seeing how you're my brother and all so for that I'm sorry. You may not forgive me now, but I hope you'll find it in your heart to one day. I know that comes with time, but I figured I'd at least put it out there."

"It's all good." James said with a slight head nod.

"So where's SJ?" I looked over at Candy

"He's staying with my Aunt until I get back."

"Oh I guess I'll see him when y'all move back here."

Don't worry Shawn it'll be soon." Shawn smiled at the thought of seeing his son then grabbed my hand.

"Thank you for such a wonderful gift."

"You're welcome." I smiled.

Chapter 6

Candy

I finally made it to Miami Florida after a long flight and I must admit it's a nice change of scenery. My cousin Tia was already at the airport when I arrived so I didn't have to wait and none of my luggage was missing so, so far the day's starting off great. "Oh my God you look so different since the last time I saw you." Tia and I embraced. "How long have you been here?"

"I got here about an hour before your flight. So you must be SJ." Tia said bending down to speak to Shawn Jr. "How old is he?"

"He just turned three." I smiled.

"Oh three, you're a big boy huh." Tia smiled as she poked his tummy causing him to laugh. "Alright then let's go we have a lot of catching up to do." Tia grabbed SJ's hand and we all headed to the exit. The ride to Tia's condo was a bit long but nice. Palm trees that lined the street were swaying from the breeze and people were rollerblading past the beautiful dark blue water that flowed along the coast. It was about 76° outside and the sun was shining, much different from the rainy weather we were having in St. Louis when I left. "So what have you been up to Tia?" I asked as I looked out the window.

"Nothing other than working. Thomas and I are looking for a house close to where we live but we haven't found much yet."

"You two have been together for a while now. How long has it been about six years?" I asked her.

"Yeah, we're engaged."

"Really, why didn't you tell me?"

"I didn't want to hear anybody's mouth about it."

"So you haven't told anybody yet?"

"Nope you're the first one. You know how Mom feels about me dating Thomas. She still refuses to meet him. I'd be lucky if he's even allowed to sit on her front porch." Tia said making a left turn.

"So what are you gonna do?"

"Keep doing what I've been doing, not listening to everybody else's opinion about who I choose to date."

"Have you met his family?" I asked curiously.

"No, they're the same way. I'm supposed to meet his sister tomorrow though. She's supposed to be more open to interracial dating. At least that's what he claims."

"So what's gonna happen when y'all get married?"

"Both of our families are just gonna have to deal with it. Our happiness is much more important than their issues about us being together."

"Well I look forward to meeting him." I smiled.

"Good cause you'll be the first one in our family that he's met," Tia smiled back.

"So are you planning on staying in Florida permanently?"

"I'm not sure. It all depends on how things work out." I replied looking on as we pulled up in a parking lot.

When I got out of the car and unstrapped SJ from his car seat, I noticed that there was a white man who looked just like Johnny Depp standing outside waiting for us. "Candy this is Thomas, Thomas this is my cousin Candy." Tia smiled.

"It's nice to finally meet you." He said as he extended his hand. I shook his hand and smiled as he politely took my bags.

"Wow polite and cute. I think you might have a winner." I whispered to Tia as we followed behind Thomas.

"So are you two hungry?" Thomas asked entering the condo.

"Yes, a little. We haven't eaten since we left this morning."

"Alright let me show you your room and then I'll order you something to eat." Thomas smiled.

"This is a big condo Tia. How many rooms are there?"

"Four in all, we turned one into an office."

"So why do you want a house?" I asked.

"We just want more room and land. Having a condo is too much like having an apartment. I'm tired of having neighbors I can hear. At least with a house I won't have that problem."

"Yeah that's true," I agreed.

After getting settled and eating, Tia and I headed out to search for jobs. "Are you sure SJ's okay staying at the house with Thomas?"

"Yes Candy he'll be fine. Thomas isn't a child molester or anything, he has a son too."

"Really, is his son's mother black?"

"No, actually I'm the first black woman he's dated," Tia replied.

"How does she act towards you?"

"Surprisingly we get along pretty well. She did warn me to be careful with him though. I don't know if she was saying that to worry me or if she was looking out for my best interest. Whatever the case, I'm keeping my guards up." A few minutes later, we pulled up to a red and white building with a parking lot full of cars. "Where are we?" I asked as we exited the car.

"This is the club I told you about, I'm cool with the manager so he said he'd give you a job."

"How do you know him?"

"We had a few classes together when I was in college. We ended up running into each other when I moved out here and we've been friends ever since." My eyes lit up with surprise from the glamorous appearance of the club when we walked in. "Wow this is beautiful, this is much nicer than the club I worked at in St. Louis."

"Welcome to Paradise." A man said with a smile as we entered.

"Hey Griffin is Winston here?" Tia asked giving the man a hug.

"Yes he just went upstairs. He should be in his office." As Tia and I went up a winding staircase I admired how exclusive and well decorated the club looked. You could definitely tell the owner put a lot of money into the place. I actually thought about giving up stripping and starting over with a clean slate, but after seeing this place, I don't know. It might be worth giving a try plus I'll probably make way more money out here than I did in St. Louis.

After walking down a nicely carpeted hallway we came to a black door with gold trim. Tia adjusted her skirt as she knocked softly. A handsome brown-skinned man with dark eyes and a neatly trimmed mustache and goatee opened the door and gestured for us to come in. "Hey Tia, how have you been."

"I'm fine how about you?" Tia replied giving him a hug and a kiss on the cheek.

"I'm good." Winston smiled.

"Well this is my cousin Candy, Candy this is Winston."

"Nice to meet you." I smiled as we shook hands. "Okay, well I'll let you two get better acquainted." Tia smiled and left the room.

"So you're Candy. Tia's told me a lot about you. I'm Winston the owner and manager of the club."

"Oh, it's nice to meet you." I smiled.

"So Tia told me you have experience. Where did you work before you moved here?" "I worked at a club called Fantasy in St. Louis for about three years." I smiled nervously. "So are you looking for part-time or full-time work?"

"I'm looking for full-time if you have it available."

"I think we can work something out, but first I need to see what you can offer this club." Winston eyeballed me from head to toe.

"Okay, what you need me to do?"

Winston walked over to the stereo that was set up in the corner of his office and pressed play. When the music started playing, he turned to me and said, "Strip." Doing as I was told, I slowly and seductively began to peel off each piece of clothing I wore as the song "Say It" by Ne-Yo blared through the speakers.

As I swiveled my hips in slow motion I noticed the look of lust on Winston's face and decided to take it a step further. I seductively walked over and straddled him, which caused him to become even more aroused. Then I began to slowly grind my pelvis into his causing him to match my speed and grind along with me. As we sat face-to-face, I stared into his eyes and held my lips so close to his that I could feel each breath he took. Just as I could feel him about to explode, he abruptly stopped me. He closed his eyes and held me still for a moment. He slowly opened his eyes and mumbled, "You got the job." A few minutes later, after he got his composure, he asked, "When can you start?"

I proudly responded, "Tonight if you want me to."

"Okay how about you come in tomorrow to fill out some paperwork and I'll have you start on Friday."

"Sounds good to me thank you Mr...."

"Just call me Winston." He interjected as he excused himself to the bathroom. Tia was standing in the hallway as I exited the office. "So what happened?"

"I got the job." I smiled.

"Cool when does he want you to start?"

"Friday, but I have to come back tomorrow to fill out some paperwork."

"Great!" Tia smiled. "Now let's go shopping." She said as we exited the building.

Chapter 7

Niki

Today is my 30th birthday and everyone but me seems to be excited about it. True enough I accomplished my dream of making partner at my law firm, but I still want more. I'm tired of working under or for people so lately I've seriously been considering opening up my own law practice. There's nothing like being your own boss. I've also been contemplating having a child eventually so my business might have to be put on the back burner for a while. It all depends on how things turn out with me and Donte. I'm not even sure that he wants kids, but I guess we'll see with time. On a positive note, Donte's taking me out to dinner for my birthday. He won't tell me where we're going so I've been on edge all day wondering what he's planned for me. After showering, I walked in my bedroom and noticed a large gold gift box on my bed with a note attached which read, *Happy birthday baby. Here's a little something to show my appreciation for you.* I quickly opened the box and pulled out a black, hand stitched lace mini-dress that I had designed, but never had time to get made. I immediately called

Donte. He answered on the first ring, "Hey baby you good?"

"Yes, I just wanted to thank you for my dress. It looks exactly how I pictured it!"

"I'm glad you like it. Now go ahead and get dressed, I'll be there to pick you up in about an hour."

"Okay baby. I love you."

"I love you too. I'll see you in a minute."

It took me half an hour to get ready. I was just finishing my hair when I heard a knock on the door. "Who is it?" I yelled as I ran downstairs. I stopped dead in my tracks when the person on the other side of the door said, "It's James."

"James?"

"Yep, you heard right."

I slowly opened the door and asked, "What are you doing here?"

"I came by to give my best wishes to the birthday girl."

"I appreciate that, but Donte will be here any minute and you know how he feels about you."

"I didn't come here to cause any trouble. I only wanted to give you a birthday gift and wish you happy birthday." He handed me a small gift box.

"Thanks James that was nice of you."

"No problem, I'm a go ahead and get out of here before Donte comes. I ain't trying to mess up your birthday so have fun." He gave me a quick hug and headed for his car. *Please hurry up and leave.* About five minutes later Donte pulled up.

"Hey baby don't worry about getting out the car, I'm ready." I yelled to Donte while locking the front door.

"You look great baby," Donte said as I got in the car.

"Thank you, where are we going?"

"That's for me to know and you to find out now sit back and enjoy the ride." A little while later we pulled up to a restaurant called Zenichay's, a nice formal restaurant that opened up not too long ago with great reviews.

"Wow Donte, this place is gorgeous. They did a great job with the restaurant." I said as a valet parked our car. "I know you've wanted to come here since it opened so I figured we'd come for your birthday."

"How'd you get reservations this place has been booked since it opened." I inquired.

"I booked them early. Plus I had some inside help."

An older woman greeted them at the door as they entered the restaurant and asked for their reservations. "It should be a table for Tillman," Donte smiled.

"Okay, your table is right this way sir." The hostess said escorting them across the room. When they arrived at the table, Charlene and Mason were already seated.

I smiled when I saw my friends. "What are you two doing here?"

"We came to celebrate your birthday with you. Now sit down so we can't eat. I'm starving." Charlene joked as she rubbed her stomach.

After ordering drinks and appetizers, we all were ready to order dinner. "So what's the special for tonight?" Charlene asked our waitress.

"We have the Chef's Special Spinelli, which is stuffed chicken breast with spinach and roasted tomatoes sprinkled with a dash of parmesan cheese. It is served with bowtie pasta marinated in a creamy garlic Alfredo sauce and served with garlic parmesan bread on the side."

"Sounds delicious. I'll have that," Charlene said licking her lips.

"We'll have the same." Everyone else agreed.

After enjoying dinner, Donte excused himself to the restroom and returned a few minutes later ready to order dessert. "Here are your menus," the waitress said as she handed a menu to each of us. "I'll give you all a moment to decide what you want." Then she winked at Donte and walked away. A few minutes later, she walked back over with a two-layer cake singing happy birthday. Talk about embarrassing, I was embarrassed as hell. I never had anyone do this before but at least I now know why the waitress was winking at my man. Oh I definitely noticed, I just didn't want to make an ass out of myself in front of all these people I'm too classy for that. After we were full of cake and ice cream, Donte stood up to propose a toast. "I'm glad the two of you were able to join us tonight for Niki's birthday especially considering Charlene needs her rest being pregnant with twins and all, congratulations by the way. Happy birthday to my baby, Niki, she's 30 years old today. Baby, I just want you to know that I love you and you've been one of the best things to happen to me since the day we met. I know I don't express my feelings often so this is why I'm telling you this." Donte walked over to me and grabbed my hand. "Baby I love you," he said as he knelt down on one knee in front of me. "We've been together for about three years now and I'm ready to take our relationship to the next level, so Niki Whitfield will you marry me?" He pulled a two-carat marquis cut diamond ring that was set in a 14-karat white gold band from his pocket. At that moment, it was as if time stood still and tears wouldn't stop forming in my eyes. "Yes I'll marry you Donte!" I finally choked out between tears. When we stood up to hug and kiss the restaurant erupted with applause while several onlookers' choked back tears.

Chapter 8

Tanya

Still shaken by the altercation with Darnell, I called Niki for comfort and advice. "Hello?" Niki answered groggily.

"Hey sis it's me."

"Tanya, are you alright?" Niki asked me with concern in her voice.

"Yeah, me and Darnelle just got into an argument."

"Do you need somewhere to stay for the night? You know you can always come here."

"No, I'm just a little upset and needed someone to talk to."

"So what happened?"

"I don't know, sometimes Darnelle can be so demanding. I'll already have a ton of things to do at home after getting off work and he'll just pile on more."

"So if you feel that way why do you do it? Tell that fool no. He needs to pull his weight too. You can't do everything by yourself that's not how a relationship's supposed to work, you share the responsibilities not pin it all on one person."

"I know Niki, I just don't feel like arguing with him. Sometimes when I try to talk to him he gets so angry to the point that it's scary."

"Tanya he didn't put his hands on you did he?"

I hesitated before I answered Niki's question. "No…"

"Tanya?" Niki called out after a brief silence.

"I'm here."

"You'd tell me if he put his hands on you wouldn't you?"

"Yeah of course I would." I lied.

"I hope so because I would hate to find out when it's too late."

"Don't worry about me sis, I'll be alright. When it comes to protecting me and Danielle I'll do whatever's necessary to make sure we're okay."

"I know you will, but you always have backup when you need it. All you gotta do is say the word and I'll be there with my gun in hand," Niki reassured.

"Oh Lord not the gun."

"Girl that's my buddy. Wherever I go she goes."

"You're a fool," I laughed.

"You need to quit playing and let me take you to get one."

"Niki I don't think I need that."

"What? Every woman needs a trusty friend. It'll make all your problems disappear literally."

"Yeah and land you in prison too," I replied still laughing.

"Oh I'm sorry I didn't make it to your birthday party tonight. I got your gift though. I'll drop it off to you tomorrow."

"It's okay, I know you're busy with Danielle and all,

besides we have even more of a reason to celebrate," Niki replied.

"Why what happened?"

"Donte proposed to me tonight."

"Oh my God! Congratulations!" Tanya screamed with excitement.

"I'm sorry I missed it."

"Don't worry you'll be able to make it up to me seeing how you'll be my maid of honor."

"Really? I'd love to! I can't wait, we have to start planning!"

Niki started laughing and said, "Tanya we haven't even decided on a date yet."

"It doesn't matter, we can at least get the small stuff out the way like the guest list, decorations, invitations, flowers, the color scheme, where you want to have it..."

"Okay, okay, I get it." Niki interrupted.

"I'm sorry, I'm just so happy for you. I'm definitely coming by tomorrow too. I have to see your ring."

"Oh it's beautiful. He did a great job picking it out." Niki said while holding up her hand to admire it.

"I have to get off the phone, but I'll call you tomorrow when I'm heading over."

"Okay take care and call me if you need anything," Niki replied.

"I will." As I hung up the phone, I noticed Darnelle standing in the doorway.

"What, you're eavesdropping on my conversations now?"

"No actually I came to apologize again for putting my hands on you and making you miss your sister's birthday gathering.

If I hadn't left everything on you to do this evening you would've been able to go… Anyway, throw on some clothes I have something to show you."

"What about Danielle? We can't just leave her here."

"She's alright. I took her over my mom's house for the night. Put something on real quick we won't be gone long." I did as he asked and threw on some clothes and followed Darnelle to the car. "Where are we going?" I asked while fastening my seatbelt.

"Just relax, you'll see," Darnelle smiled.

Thirty minutes later, we pulled up to a park. After parking the car, Darnelle grabbed a duffle bag from the back seat and got out. I looked at the bag curiously. "What's that?"

"Nothing, just come on," Darnelle replied. After finding a nice secluded spot in the grass by the lake, he pulled a blanket out of the duffle bag and spread it across the grass. He gestured to me saying, "Have a seat." Then he lit two candles and sat down beside me. "Look up," he said pointing at the stars. "What do you feel?"

"Peace." I replied.

"Exactly, that's what I want you to feel all the time. I don't want us to be at each other's throat constantly. I know it's hard being with me sometimes especially having to deal with my attitude, but I am trying to work on it.

"I know, but I don't feel like you're working hard enough. I'm tired of risking being hit every time we argue. I shouldn't have to feel scared in my own house, especially of the one person who's supposed to love me."

"I know Tanya and I'm sorry for that. I promise you I won't put my hands on you again."

"You sure won't because the next time you do I'm taking

Danielle and leaving."

"I understand." Darnelle raised his hands in submission. Then he reached inside his bag and took out a teddy bear holding a box of almond Hershey's Kisses, a dozen long stemmed roses, and a card that read *I'm sorry.*

To say I was surprised was an understatement. Darnelle had really gone all out this time. "When did you get this?"

"When you were talking on the phone to your sister. Will you forgive me?"

"Yes Darnelle." I leaned over and kissed him on the lips as he caressed my leg. Wiping away tears that formed in my eyes, Darnelle caressed my cheek then leaned me back on the blanket and kissed me passionately. Darnelle slowly slid his hand up my skirt and whispered I love you.

"I love you too," As I reached up to take off Darnelle's shirt a bright light flashed in my face. "What the hell!" I yelled, blinded by the light.

"'I guess I came just in time." A police officer said with a smile on his face. "I swear people like you make my job worthwhile, gives me something to do."

"That's nice and all, but you think you can get that light out of my face." I said as I held my hand over my eyes.

"I need you two to come with me." The officer said pointing his flashlight at Darnelle. Doing as they were told Tanya and Darnelle followed the officer to his police car for questioning. "So is there any particular reason why you two are out here this late at night?"

"We came here to relax. We wanted to get out the house and I thought this would be a nice quiet place to do it," Darnelle responded.

"It didn't look like that's what you two were doing. It looked like you were about to have sex in a public park, which is a fine up to a thousand dollars. Now I'm gonna let you off with a warning this time, but if it happens again you're going to jail and I guarantee you there will be a hefty fine attached to it. Is that understood?"

"Yes officer and thank you." I said happy to get off with a warning.

"Alright then, you two run along and don't let this happen again." The officer pulled off in his squad car and we headed home feeling like two teenagers who'd been caught in the act.

The following morning I headed into work happy that we didn't get thrown in jail. The moment I walked into the office I noticed Shelly wasn't at her desk, as usual, and there was a large bouquet of roses sitting on top of it. "Humph, I wonder who those are from?" Being nosey, I walked over to her desk and decided to take a peek at the card attached to them.

Shelly baby I didn't mean what I said the other day. You are very important to me and I don't want to lose you so hopefully this will make up for everything I said to you.

My sincerest apologies,
　　　　C.C. (Carlton Conway)

Humph, ain't that something? You'd think the man didn't have a wife and kids at home. I quickly took the card out of the bouquet of flowers for evidence and headed back to my desk. The moment my butt hit the seat Mrs. Conway came strolling through the door. Mrs. Conway is a tall slender woman with long brunette hair that she wore layered. She was always a kind, fashionable woman and today wasn't any different. She wore a fitted skirt that flared slightly above the knee with a matching jacket and a purple silk blouse with the top three buttons undone. She topped it off with a pair of peep toe pumps that strapped around the ankle and accentuated her long legs. "Good morning Tanya, how have you been?" She smiled.

"Pretty good and how about you?"

"I'm well, just busy as usual. What about Niki, she still practicing law?"

"Yes, you know she's getting married." I smiled.

"Oh really? Tell her congratulations for me and I'll be looking forward to the invite."

"I sure will."

"Is my husband here?" At that moment, I had a good mind to tell her he's probably out somewhere screwing Shelly but I opted against it, eventually the truth will come out.

"He should be in his office."

"Ok, thanks Tanya." As she headed back to his office, I continued filing papers. I was interrupted by a loud commotion a couple of minutes later. Sliding out of my seat, I peeked around the corner to see what was going on. *He must've gotten caught.* I thought to myself with a sly grin. Against my better judgment, I walked down the hall and into Mr. Conway's office. I found him naked and standing in the middle of the floor holding a stack of papers over his private. Shelley, on the other hand, was lying on top of his desk with nothing on being choked by Mrs. Conway.

I ran in to break up the altercation and literally had to pry

Mrs. Conway's hands off of Shelley's neck. "You fucking whore! You sat there and smiled in my face every day I came up here knowing full well you were sleeping with my husband you cheap skank!" Mrs. Conway lunged at Shelley with a stapler in her hand.

"Honey please! I'm sorry!" Mr. Conway said jumping in the middle of them.

"You sure are you sorry son of a bitch!" Mrs. Conway yelled as the palm of her hand landed across his face, causing his cheek to turn a bright shade of red.

"How long has this been going on huh?"

"Honey please!" Mr. Conway replied.

"How long Carlton, how long have you been sleeping with this whore?" Mrs. Conway drew her hand back to slap him again.

"It started a couple of weeks after she got here."

"So the whole seven or eight months she's been here you've been fucking her then bringing your sorry ass home to me!"

"He's divorcing you! Didn't he tell you? He already sent you the papers in the mail." Shelly interjected with a smirk on her face.

"You lousy home wrecking bitch!" Mrs. Conway lunged at Shelly and managed to grab a fist full of her hair. She pulled as hard she could in an attempt to yank her backwards.

"Let me go!" Shelly yelled as she kicked and clawed hoping to connect with Mrs. Conway.

"Honey stop you're going to hurt her!" Mr. Conway pled.

"I know that's the point asshole." Ms. Conway said as she slapped him in the head for getting in the way. Mr. Conway looked at me with a shameful expression on his face and lowered his head as he attempted to cover his nudity. I guess with all the commotion going on he hadn't had a chance to put his clothes back on. Looking at him with disgust, I shook my head and decided to help him pry the two women apart.

"Honey I'm sorry, I really am. Please can we at least talk about this?"

"There's nothing to talk about, you made your bed so now you lay in it. I'll see you in court." Mrs. Conway spat then stormed out the office.

Itching to tell somebody what had just happened so I rushed back to my desk. I was digging through my purse for my cell phone to call Niki when Mr. Conway stormed over to my desk. "What did you do?" He spat with a grimace on his.

"Excuse me!" I was shocked. I couldn't believe this fool had the nerve to try to blame his fuck up on me. He should've been better at concealing his business, besides, I'm not the one who made him lay down with Shelly that was his own decision so the only person he has to blame for what happened is himself.

"Did you call her up here?"

"No I didn't and I don't appreciate you…"

"Let me tell you something bitch, if I lose my family over this I swear before God I'm gonna hang your ass alive and I'll see to it that you never work again. I promise you with every bone in my body I'll have your ass standing in the welfare line faster than you can blink!"

Before I could get a word out he had already stormed back into his office and slammed the door. Though I was in total shock I had every intention to go give him a piece of my mind, but I stopped in my tracks when I heard the front door opening. Assuming it was a client I spun around on my heels while mentally preparing an excuse to get whomever it was to leave. "Niki." I smiled and let out a sigh of relief.

"How long have you been standing out there?"

"Long enough to hear everything my husband just said to you." Ms. Conway interjected, walking in behind Niki.

"I thought you left?"

"I did. I came back to get his house keys back, after today he won't be needing them." Mrs. Conway smirked. "So what else has happened in my absence?" Mrs. Conway asked me.

I explained how Mr. Conway promoted Shelly over me and other issues I'd been experiencing in the office.

"Don't worry I will personally see to it that he compensates you for all he's put you through. I need to know one thing though." Mrs. Conway said leaning against the doorway. "Did you ever catch them fooling around here in the office?"

"Yes, yesterday I walked in on them having sex on top of his desk and threatened to tell you and call the Better Business Bureau on him but you caught him before I could say anything."

Mrs. Conway shook her head with her hand on her chest. I think she was too angry to cry because she took my response rather lightly..

"Mrs. Conway are you alright?" I asked her concerned.

"Yes dear I'm fine. I had a feeling something was going on all this time I just didn't want to face it. But at least now I know the truth.

"So are they still in his office?" Niki asked with her face frowned up. I could tell my sis was mad from her expression. Niki was never good at hiding her feelings her face always told everything she was thinking.

"Yes, they're still back there."

"Okay." Niki marched down the hallway to his office followed by Mrs. Conway and I. We stood outside the door and listened to the two of them arguing.

"Did you call my wife?"

"Did you send the divorce papers?" Shelly replied.

"Answer my question!" Mr. Conway demanded.

"When you answer mine. Did you mail her the divorce papers?"

"Do you realize what I have at stake here?" Mr. Conway rubbed his hands across his face irritated.

"Do you realize what I had at stake? I left my husband for you because you said you were going to get a divorce!"

"Humph, ain't that something?" Mrs. Conway cracked the door open and stood there with a smirk and her arms crossed.

Mr. Conway turned to the doorway with a surprised look on his face. "How long have you been standing there?"

"Honey I don't think you're in the position to be asking questions." Mrs. Conway said while leaning against the doorframe. "Now answer her question Carlton. Did you mail the papers? Because I'm interested in knowing too."

"No I didn't," he mumbled.

"You son of a bitch!" Shelly yelled as she pounded him wildly with her fists. "You liar! I hate you! I lost my husband because of you!"

"You lost your husband because of you I never told you to leave your husband." Mr. Conway replied while grabbing her arms to keep from getting hit.

"Since you told me the truth I guess it's only right that I

tell you the truth Carlton." Shelly said with a sadistic smile on her face. "I'm the one who called your wife. I told you payback is a bitch! Oh and one more thing, I'm HIV positive." At that point, all hell broke loose. Mr. Conway tried to choke the life out of that woman while poor Mrs. Conway just stood in the doorway stunned and holding her chest as tears rolled down her cheeks. True enough Shelly and Mr. Conway got what they deserved, but I didn't need no murders happening in front of me so me and Niki pulled Mr. Conway off Shelly and watched as she gasped for air. After clearing up the commotion, I watched as Mrs. Conway calmly walked over to Mr. Conway while he stood with his head in his hands crying. She stared at him momentarily then hit him as hard as she could over and over again with a stapler she got off his desk, until she drew blood.

"You bastard!" She yelled as we pulled her off him. "Let me go I'm calm." Mrs. Conway pulled away from us and adjusted her skirt. "I swear as God is my witness you will never see me or your kids again. And bitch if I find out I have HIV when I go to the doctor tomorrow I'm gonna pay somebody to kill your ass. I put that on my life. If you think I'm joking you'll know for sure when the cops find your dead body floating down the Mississippi River!" Then she turned to Mr. Conway and gave him a look of disgust before saying, "As for you my dear husband... as of today you've been evicted!" She threw her wedding ring at him, took the key to their house and car out his desk drawer and walked out.

"Now we're equal." Shelly smirked then sashayed out the office.

Mr. Conway looked from me to Niki and shook his head. "Tanya will you cancel all of my meetings and appointments for today I'm really not in the mood for clients."

"Who me?" I said while looking around as if he were talking to someone else.

"Of course you who else would I be talking to."

"Not me, I quit. Get your own damn calls or call Shelly and have her do it. I'm sure she won't mind. Good luck with your issues." I laughed then walked out.

"Oh and by the way, you will be receiving a subpoena from my client to appear in court for discrimination and harassment. I'll be sure to have the cops personally deliver it to your office. Have a blessed day Mr. Conway." Niki said with a smile before leaving.

Mr. Conway stood in the middle of his office staring at the door as he wallowed in his own misery. "All of this is my fault; it's all my fault," he said to himself repeatedly.

Chapter 9

Niki

I'm at work handling some files I had left over from the day before and all of a sudden Candy tells me I have a call. "Go ahead and put it through," I said thinking it was Donte or one of my clients.

"Good morning, Whitfield and Bates Law Firm, this is Ms. Whitfield."

"Why did you put a restraining order against me?"

"How did you get through to my secretary?"

"Let's just say I know someone that knows someone."

"What the hell do you want, Shawn?"

"What do you mean what do I want? I want my woman back."

"Well, good luck with that happening. You should've thought about that before you cheated on me."

"Give me a chance to make it right," Shawn pled.

"After all you've done and put me through? Hell, no!"

"Baby, wait! Don't hang up. I sent you something!"

Before he could finish talking I hung up on him. The next thing you know I heard a knock on my door, and as I opened it, in comes a singing telegram with a basket of flowers, candy, and teddy bears. I politely gave the delivery boy a tip and sent him on his way, but he refused to take the basket back with him so I was stuck with it. I ate a couple pieces of the candy and pulled out the card.

"I AM TRULY SORRY FOR ALL I'VE PUT YOU THROUGH AND WOULD LIKE FOR YOU TO FORGIVE ME. I WANT YOU BACK. I MISS YOU, BABY, PLEASE COME BACK. I STILL LOVE YOU!"

At that point all I could do was laugh. He was truly a character. First, he cheats on me and threatens to hit me. Then, he tries to rape me, and now he has the nerve to say he loves me. I would toss this whole basket at his head if I saw him. Speaking of the devil, guess who busts through my door? I immediately tossed the whole basket at his head, which slightly grazed his face. *Man, I gotta get better aim,* I thought to myself.

"How the hell did you get past Security, and why are you locking my door?" Niki asked as she walked over and unlocked the door.

"I don't have time to explain," Shawn said out of breath. "I just wanted to see and talk to you."

Immediately I called Security.

"Baby, look, I just wanna talk."

"I don't wanna hear it! Get out of my office!"

Then I heard another knock on the door.

"Come in!" I yelled. "Candy, is Security on their way?"

"Yes," Candy replied. Looking over to her right Candy lowered her eyes to a glare.

"Shawn, what are you doing here? You know him, Ms.

Whitfield?"

"Yes," Niki replied.

"That's the guy at the bachelor's party I was telling you about."

"Candy told you about the bachelor's party?" Shawn asked.

"Yes," Niki responded.

"I didn't know he was your fiancé or I would've said something sooner," Candy replied.

"Bitch, I knew it was you that told her. That's why she won't take me back!"

"Oh no, Shawn! Don't try to blame this on her! You're the one that fucked up! *You're* the reason it's over!"

Then we heard a pounding on the door.

"Who is it?"

"It's Security."

"Come in," I yelled.

"We're looking for that man right there. We had him apprehended, but somehow he managed to break loose."

"Please take him out of here."

"Yes, ma'am, and we're sorry for our negligence."

"Thank you," Niki replied.

Candy pulled up a chair and sat down looking concerned. "I am so sorry. I honestly didn't know he was your fiancé."

"Don't worry about it. I'm just glad it happened before I made the mistake of marrying him. That just opened up the gates for a better man," Niki replied.

That evening I went home and called Donte. After telling him everything that happened he was furious. "I gotta do something about this cat and fast," Donte said.

Chapter 10

Ariel, Donte, and Niki

I remember that day like it was yesterday. The moment I stepped in the house and Mason came rushing towards me with bags in his hands. "Where are you going?" I looked at him with my eyebrows raised.

"Out," he said then pushed pass me.

"What you mean out?"

Mason turned on his heels and got in my face. "Don't start questioning me. You should be the last person asking me anything."

"Mason I said I was sorry, we can do something today if you want to.

"Nah I'm good," he said continuing towards the door.

"How long are you gonna be gone?"

"I don't know."

"Why don't you know, who are you staying with? Is it another woman?" I asked, but he ignored me so I grabbed his arm. "It is isn't it?"

"Let me go so I can leave. I got things to do." Mason replied irritated.

"Mason please don't leave I said I'm sorry." He snatched his arm from my grip and stared at me briefly then headed for his car. "What do I need to do to make this right? Please Mason talk to me!" I pled as I followed behind him.

"Seriously I just can't be around you right now. I'll come back after I calm down."

"But Mason I'm sorry." I said with tears in my eyes as I attempted to grab him again.

"Don't touch me. I'm not in the mood for that right now." He said as he looked at me as if I had a disease. "I'll holla at you later."

"Mason please!" He ignored my cries and sped out of the driveway and down the street leaving nothing but a trail of dust. After watching Mason's car disappear down the block I broke down in tears and rushed to call Dana.

"Hello." Dana answered sounding out of breath.

"Hey, did I call at a bad time?"

"Nah you good, what's up?"

"Mason left," I told her while sniffing back tears.

"What you mean he left? Was it for good?"

"I don't know. He was pretty upset. I just don't know what to do." I sobbed.

"Girl I told you to quit playing with that man. There's only so much a man like that will put up with." Dana replied not surprised by the news.

"What should I do? He said he'd come back once he's calmed down."

"Well, let him be girl. Don't keep bothering him because you're just gonna piss him off even more. If he needs a moment give him that moment."

"But what if he's with another woman?" I asked worried.

"Were you not with another man? That's really the last thing you should be worried about. You should be more worried about him staying gone forever if you pissed him off the way you said you did."

"I know I just want him to come home," I whined.

"He will just give him time." After a brief silence, Dana spoke again. "Look I gotta go so I'll call you later to see how you're doing ok."

"Okay, thanks Dana."

"Anytime girl, now stop crying and get yourself together. Everything will be alright just have faith."

That night I stayed up until four o'clock in the morning hoping Mason would come home. I kept jumping up and running to the window every time I heard a car come down the street thinking it might be him, but he never showed up. It took me doing that at least five or six times before I finally realized I was fooling myself, so I crawled under my covers and cried myself to sleep.

After a week had passed without hearing a word from Mason, I got tired of moping around and decided to go out and get some fresh air. I got up around nine in the morning, took a shower, combed my hair, picked out something comfortable to wear, and headed out the door. No sooner than I stepped outside my phone rang. Hoping it was Mason, I quickly picked up the phone. "Hey baby what you up to?" Keith asked sounding happy to hear my voice.

"Nothing just stepping out to get some fresh air." "How did things go with your dude when you made it home?"

"He hasn't been home since that day. He was heading out the door as soon as I walked in."

"Damn I'm sorry baby, you alright?"

"Yeah I'm good. I did kinda bring this on myself."

"That's true," Keith agreed.

"Well damn thanks for agreeing."

"Anytime baby, anytime." I laugh a little at his joke. "So what are we gonna do today?" Keith asked me.

"Who said I was hanging with you, the last time I checked *I* was going out for fresh air I didn't say *we*."

"Come on let me take you out for breakfast."

"It's like noon now don't you think it's a little late for breakfast?"

"Fine let's do lunch then."

"I don't know Keith." I hesitated.

"Come on you know you wanna go. It'll get your mind off things for a while." After a brief silence, I agreed. "Okay I guess, but that's it only lunch."

"Alright, where you wanna meet?" Keith asked.

"Donny's, the waffle house off the highway."

"Sounds good to me, give me a half an hour." Keith said happy that I agreed.

After hanging up with Keith I headed straight to the restaurant so I'd be on time. It usually only takes me about fifteen minutes to get there but traffic can be a bitch around this time a day so I knew I'd need the extra time. Keith was already seated when I arrived and gestured for me to come over. As I sat down, I admired his toned arms in the black t-shirt he wore. True enough he was dressed down compared to the night we met but he was still just as sexy if not sexier.

"Hey you made it." Keith said as he stood up to pull out my chair.

Oh how nice, a gentleman. "How long have you been here?"

"Not long only about fifteen minutes. I took the liberty of ordering our drinks. I got you a sweet tea to start with."

"That's cool." I began looking through my menu.

"So your man still ain't come back yet?" Keith asked curious.

"No, but it's my fault so I can't really be mad at him."

"So do you still love him?" Keith asked taking a sip of his lemonade.

"Yes I love him. I just get frustrated with him sometimes."

"Ariel don't take this the wrong way, but if that's so why did you spend the night with me?"

"Because I was drunk and tripping." I replied avoiding eye contact.

"Why do people always try to blame it on the liquor? You were drunk but I'm sure you were aware of what you were doing. Just admit the truth. You did it because you wanted to."

"No I did it because I was drunk." I reiterated.

"Yeah keep telling yourself that but we both know the truth."

I knew the truth, but I didn't feel like hearing it from Keith. "Look, did we come here for you to quiz me or eat?"

"No need to get mad, I was just want to know why you

allowed things to go as far as you did."

"Ummm, these waffles look good." I tried changing the subject.

"I get you, if you don't wanna talk about it that's cool." Keith smirked. After enjoying our breakfast, we headed over to Keith's place to watch a movie. "Are you comfortable coming over here after the last incident?"

"I think I'll be ok besides, I could use some company right now." I smiled. Once we got in the house, I kicked my shoes off and plopped down on the sofa.

"You comfortable?" Keith grinned.

"Why yes I am, now may I have something to drink?"

"Yeah let me see what I got." Keith said as he headed towards the kitchen. I tapped him on the shoulder as he rummaged through the refrigerator for something to drink and startled him.

"Sorry, I didn't mean to scare you. I couldn't find any good movies on TV."

"It's okay, you play cards?"

"Of course I do." I smiled.

"You any good at spades?"

"I sure am."

"Alright then let's see." Keith pulled a deck of cards out the kitchen drawer and began shuffling them. He had me cut them and dealt both of us a hand. After playing for about an hour and winning two out of three games Keith decided to make it interesting. "Alright for every game you lose you have to do whatever I ask and if I lose…"

"You'll have to do what I ask." I interjected giving him a devilish grin. The first game we played Keith won. "Since I won you have to answer my question."

"What question?" I shifted in my seat.

"The one you avoided at the restaurant."

"Fine. Yes, I knew it was a chance something could happen between us, but I figured I could handle it. Things went much further than they were supposed to and now because of my dumb decision I may have lost my husband." A feeling of sorrow and regret washed over me as I replayed the events of that night.

"Just because he left doesn't mean he's not coming back. He probably just needs some time to sort things out." Keith replied sympathetic. After a brief silence, Keith smiled. "Come on it's your deal." He said handing me the cards. After losing another round of spades, I decided it was time to go home.

"You owe me one more thing before you leave." Keith said staring at me.

"And what's that?"

"A Kiss." Keith smiled.

"That's probably not a good idea."

"I won so it's only fair, we made a bet." Keith teased.

"One kiss and that's it then I'm heading home." I slowly moved towards him. Expecting to give Keith a quick peck on the lips I closed my eyes and kissed him softly but before I could break free Keith pulled me in closer. Gently holding the back of my head, he kissed me more passionately then slid his hand down my back and around my waist. Feeling Keith's arousal tempted me to do more so I quickly pulled away. "I think I need to go home."

"You sure?" Keith said as he pulled me back into him and softly kissed my neck. I closed my eyes and enjoyed the warmth of Keith's breath on my neck as he kissed my earlobe.

"Yes I'm sure... I have to leave." Hesitantly I slowly pulled away once more.

"Alright baby, call me when you get home." Keith looked at me disappointed." As I walked to my car, I fought the urge to go back and finish what we started. It was hard as hell to leave but I knew what would happen if I stayed.

When I got home Mason's car was in the driveway. Excited, I hurried to get in the house in hopes that I could get him to talk to me. "Mason!" I called out as I went from room to room but I didn't receive an answer. I found him in the bedroom packing up more clothes. "Mason," I said softly as I stepped closer to him. "Are you staying?"

"Does it look like I'm staying?" Mason sarcastically spat as he continued to place clothes in his bag. "Mason look at me!" I said trying to get his attention. I started crying and began pleading with him. "Please don't go Mason I need you." He finally made eye contact and stared at me briefly then wiped one of my tears away with his finger. "You don't love me anymore?" I asked looking at him.

"Yes, I still love you. I'm just a little upset still. Just give me a little time, I'll be back." After watching him pack a few more clothes, I followed him to the front door and sighed. "Don't worry I'll be back I just got a few things I need to handle. I'll be at Donte's spot if you need anything okay." Then he gave me a peck on the lips and headed to his car.

A little while later, I sat on my couch with the TV playing. I was lost in thought until the phone rang and snapped me out of my trance. "Hey girl, you alright?" Dana asked concerned.

"Yeah I'm good."

"Did he come home yet?"

"He just left."

"Did he say anything to you?"

"At first no, but he started to warm up to me a little after a while. He told me he had a few things he needed to handle and that he'd be at his friend's house if I need him."

"Well that's a good start." Dana said hoping for the best. "Did he say he'd be back?"

"Yeah, he said just give him a little time."

"Then there's nothing to worry about as long as he said he's coming back." Dana replied.

"Yeah that's true."

"Why do you sound so disappointed, isn't this what you wanted?"

"Yeah but I have another issue, I haven't come on my cycle yet for this month."

"Please don't tell me you didn't use protection with that dude," Dana said sounding disappointed.

"Honestly I don't remember, everything happened so fast and I wasn't thinking."

"Have you had cramps or anything?" Dana asked sounding worried.

"Yes."

"Then maybe the date is changing or something, how many days has it been since you were supposed to come on?"

"Only two or three days."

"Give it a minute then, now if next month comes and you haven't come on yet then you may have a problem on your hands."

"Yeah I know, I usually don't come on till around the end

of the month. It changed dates not too long ago and the same thing happened so that could be the case this time too."

"All we can do now is wait and see," Dana replied with a sigh. "Well I gotta go pick up Shana from her father's house 'cause you know it's my week to have her, so I'll give you a call tomorrow."

"Okay, thank you for listening to all my problems I know it gets annoying sometimes." I said with a smile.

"You're good. You know I'm here for you if you need me. I'd rather you dump all your problems out on me than keep them all bottled in until you explode. I know how that is. I've done it before and believe me it ain't pretty. I'll talk to you later though." Dana said then hung up. Well I guess I gotta wait it out. There's no point of wasting money on a pregnancy test if I'm not pregnant.

Niki

Since the engagement, I've been so excited that I can't even sleep. I can't believe I'm finally getting married! I thought this day would never come. I started planning our wedding the moment Donte got down on his knee. I don't want to wait too long to get married because I want to have kids and at 29 years old my clock is ticking. I wasn't thrilled with the idea of having kids out of wedlock so from the looks of it everything's gonna go as planned. As for the wedding itself, I don't want to rush and put it together so we decided to wait at least a year to make sure there's plenty of time to plan it.

I was rushing to meet my planner hoping she wouldn't beat me to the restaurant. I almost ran a red light frantically dialing my sister Tanya's number. "Oh shit!" I said stomping down on my brakes causing my car to come to a screeching halt.

"Niki?" Tanya's voice echoed through my speakerphone.

"Hello, oh I'm sorry Tanya." I said scrambling to pull my phone from in between my car seat.

"Niki are you alright?"

"Girl I almost ran a red light."

"You sound like you're doing too much at one time."

"Yeah I am. I wanna make sure I'm there on time to meet the planner. Are you there already?" I asked as I fumbled around for my earpiece.

"Yeah I'm here so you're good. If she comes before you get here I'll keep her company."

"Okay, thank you Tanya."

"No problem, you just need to slow down before you have an accident. Take your time I'm here." Tanya reassured.

"Alright I'll be there in a minute." Knowing that Tanya was there already made me feel more at ease. I slowed down a bit and went over our wedding plans in my head. When I arrived, Tanya and my wedding planner, Cynthia, were sitting at a table talking. Cynthia was a brown-skinned woman who was in her early fifties, but looked like she was no more than 41 or 42. Her skin was smooth and flawless. She was a petite but pretty woman and you could tell she was a knockout in her younger days.

"Come on over," Tanya mouthed as she gestured for me to join them.

"Hey, sorry I'm a little late there was a bit of traffic." I said as I reached over to shake Cynthia's hand.

"Oh it's fine I just got here myself." Cynthia said with a

soothing voice and calming demeanor that reminded me a lot of my mother and helped me relax a bit. Then she went straight to the business at hand and began asking about our plans. "So do you already have an idea of how you want your wedding or are we starting from scratch?"

"I have some ideas that I wrote down, but I'm not sure what color scheme I want to go for."

"Okay, well I have a few color charts and pictures of other weddings I've done so you can get an idea of how the colors will be put together for the wedding. Are you planning on a big wedding?" Cynthia asked with a warm smile.

"No. Somewhat small, but not too small. I plan on having 100 to 150 guests, including the wedding party."

"Have you put together a guest list yet?"

"Yes, but I have to confirm everyone."

"It's really early so there's no rush." Cynthia calmly stated as she took a sip of her water.

After going over a few more ideas about the color scheme of the wedding and photos of various venues, I decided to do a little more research before making a final decision.

"Well I guess we're done for now," Cynthia said while getting her things together. "My assistant, Layla, will be giving you a call tomorrow to set up an appointment for the two of you to meet. She'll be working closely with me to get things done so I would like you to meet her."

"Okay, that sounds good" I replied excited to start the planning process.

"Alright then. I'll be in touch and I look forward to working with you." We shook hands and then Cynthia headed for the door. After getting the remainder of our food put in to-go boxes, Tanya and I headed to our cars.

"Looks like I got a lot to do sis." I said nervously.

"Don't worry, that's the point of having a planner, to take the burden off you."

"I know. I just hope her assistant is as easy going as she is." What I liked about her most was that she was kind, very professional, and easy to talk to so naturally I felt more at ease about the wedding. I can only pray that me and her assistant Layla click as well as we did.

"I'm sure everything will be fine," Tanya said as she gave me a hug goodbye.

The next morning I received a phone call from Layla and we agreed to meet around one o'clock at Shay's Café, a small diner located in a shopping plaza about twenty minutes away from my home. Since Donte was off work he agreed to come with me. This made me happy because I wouldn't have to drive. When we arrived at the café I headed to the restroom while Donte stood out front and waited for Layla. When I stepped out the restroom, I noticed a dark-skinned woman in a tan pants suit flirting with Donte. She was about 5'8" with shoulder-length dark brown hair. I briskly walked over and grabbed Donte by his hand. Donte smiled and introduced the woman, "Hey baby, this is Layla."

"Oh hi, you must be Niki." Layla said while extending her hand for me to shake. "We spoke over the phone a couple of times, I'm Cynthia's assistant."

"Yes, I remember. I see you've met my husband, Donte," I said giving a fake smile.

"Oh yes and he is quite the charmer."

"I'm so sure he is." I said cutting my eyes at her as she eyed Donte as if he were an entrée. I was ready to slap the taste out of Ms. Layla's mouth so I was happy when the waitress finally called us to be seated. If I had to sit there one more minute watching that bitch eyeballing my man I may have actually hurt her.

We shared an awkward silence for a moment after placing our drink orders. Layla broke the silence by asking, "So have you two already decided on a wedding date?"

"No not yet, we're still deciding."

"Has Cynthia gone over the wedding theme and photos with you already?"

"Yes we went over them yesterday. She told me she wanted us to meet you since you would be assisting her with our wedding," I replied dryly.

Layla turned her focus towards Donte and smiled. "So Donte do you have any ideas? I know Niki's not doing all the planning alone."

"No I don't, I'm leaving most of the planning up to Niki and her sister. Plus that's the reason we hired you and Mrs. Cynthia."

"Well you got a point and I guarantee you will be very pleased with the final results. Anyway, since Cynthia's already gone over most of the details regarding the wedding I guess I should let you know my role in this." Layla said while looking at me. "My full name is Layla Haywood and my job is to fill in wherever Cynthia needs me. I will mostly be taking care of things such as your flower arrangements and decorations. Also, I'll be here to help if either of you have any questions or concerns and Cynthia is unavailable." She pulled out two business cards and handed them to me and

Donte. "Have you already chosen a place for the wedding?"

"I have a few places in mind, but I haven't made a final decision yet. Lately I've just been checking to see what dates they have available to help narrow down my choices." I said hoping that this meeting would be over soon.

"Okay, well there's not much more we need to do so I guess we'll be giving you a call." Layla said with a fake smile as she stood up to shake our hands. As she reached over to shake Donte's hand, she flirted with her eyes and lingered with her handshake. Donte looked at her as if she were crazy and snatched his hand away. Then he turned to me and told me he'd wait for me in the car.

"So how long have you been working for Cynthia?" I asked curiously.

"About a year maybe, why?" Layla asked dryly.

"I was just curious so I figured I'd ask."

After the meeting with Layla Donte and I decided to head over to see Mason and Charlene. Charlene was outside sitting on the porch when we drove up.

I greeted Charlene and gave her a hug. "Where's Mason?"

"Inside the house watching the basketball game. Hey Donte." Charlene said as Donte walked up behind me.

"What's up, where Mason at?"

"In the living room watching the game."

"Good we got a bet we need to finish."

"No betting!" I yelled behind Donte as he walked towards the house.

"Girl that's what they do, believe me it gets on my nerves to. So how was the wedding planner?" Charlene asked as we sat out on the porch.

"Cynthia seems nice, but I don't like her assistant."

"What's wrong with her?" Charlene laughed.

"The bitch couldn't stop eyeing my man."

"Oh she one of those huh?"

"Yep, that's why I wanna get her ass fired. Cuz she got one more time to look at me sideways and I promise you we gone have it out."

"Is she that bad?" Charlene asked trying not to laugh again.

"Yes she is."

"So what you gonna do?"

"I don't know yet, but if she keeps testing me I'm gonna fire her ass personally."

"You silly Niki," Charlene said laughing.

"I'm serious, that's disrespectful and unprofessional. It's one thing to admire or glance at my man, but it's another to be staring him down like a Thanksgiving dinner."

After getting up to grab a couple glasses of lemonade Charlene sat down and handed one to me. "So have you decided what color scheme you want to use for the wedding yet?"

"I think I'm gonna go with a chocolate brown and salmon or floral pink color."

"That sounds nice," Charlene agreed.

"Speaking of which, are you free tomorrow? I want you and Tanya to come with me to shop for my wedding dress and your bridesmaid gowns."

"I have a doctor's appointment in the morning, but I should be home around one o'clock."

"Okay that's sounds good. I can't wait!" I said with excitement.

"Me either I'm happy for you," Charlene smiled.

Donte

"What's up, I ain't seen you in a while?" Mason and I gave each other dap.

"Man I been chillin. Since Char got pregnant, she needs my help around the house more. I don't want her stressin about nothing. She needs to be taking it easy."

"Yeah that's true. I've been going through the same thing with this wedding and all. Niki hasn't asked me to do much, but I try to pitch in every now and then so she won't think I don't care."

"So when are we going to pick out our tuxes?" Mason asked sitting down and handing me a beer.

"We can go tomorrow if you got some free time. Plus I spoke to Tyrone yesterday. He said him and some of the dudes are meeting up around two to play a couple games of basketball. If we head out early maybe we can make it in time to get in on the game."

"That's a bet. I haven't played in a minute so I'm ready to get back on the court." Mason replied taking a sip of his beer. "So how you feeling about getting married, the cold feet catch up to you yet?"

"Nah I'm good, I'm just ready to gone and do it. I hate all the anticipation. Had she left it up to me we would've gone to the Justice of the Peace. She's the one that wanted to have the big wedding ceremony so I'm just going along for the ride."

"Yeah I feel you." Mason agreed.

"What about you, how you holding up with Char being pregnant and all?"

"I'm cool. I'm actually looking forward to being a father. I always wanted another kid and this time I think I picked the right woman to have one with." Mason smiled proudly.

"So when do you have to go to divorce court?"

"The day after tomorrow, then I'll be officially divorced from that hoe. I can't wait!" Mason exclaimed.

"Did she ever find out who Nate's father is?"

"I don't know. I haven't spoke to her since the results came back. That was some foul shit she did so after that I told her don't call me no more."

"And she actually listened?" I laughed.

"Yeah she don't have no reason to call me without Nate involved."

"I'm about to get up outta here cuz we got a few more runs to make." I got up to give Mason dap. "Don't forget we heading out around ten tomorrow and I haven't forgot you still owe me for that bet."

"What bet?" Mason looked at me confused.

"The one we made when me and Niki first got together. Remember when I told you I was gonna end up marrying her."

"Aww man you was serious about that? I thought we was just talking." Mason grinned slightly.

"Yeah ok, that was fifty dollars' worth of talking we agreed on so all that's left is for you to pay up."

"Damn I thought you forgot about that."

"Nope I remember like it was yesterday."

"Y'all ain't officially married yet so see me after the wedding."

"Alright that's fair, but don't act like you forgot when I hold my hand out for my money."

"You got it." Mason said laughing as we walked towards the door. "I'll holla at you tomorrow."

An hour later Niki and I were out running a few errands. "Baby let me see that card Layla gave you. I can't find the one she gave me and I need her number." Niki said shuffling through her purse.

"Here you go. It's in the first compartment of my wallet." Niki examined the business card Layla gave me and then she looked at me with her face frowned up.

"Did you know this shit was on here?"

"What shit?" I asked confused as I took the card out of her hand. The front of the card displayed Layla's business information but she had written her phone number and a note that read, *hit me up when you get a chance* on the back.

"I know that bitch didn't think she could get away with that one!"

"Baby calm down maybe she gave me the wrong card." I said attempting to soothe the situation.

"Wrong card my ass! That skank knew what she was doing! I knew all along that she was out to get you. I could tell by the way she was looking at you! See men be trying to play dumb, but y'all know when these women are hitting on you." Niki rolled her eyes.

"Man I didn't know she wrote that shit on the back of the card. It's not like I asked her for her number she did that on her own."

"I know that, I'm just pissed that the heffa would be that bold to give you her number while I'm sitting there with you. She could've at least waited until I went to the restroom or something. I'm finna call her ass right now. I should put you on the phone to see what she says." Niki said as she punched Layla's number in her cell phone.

"Don't do that baby." I pled.

"Why not?"

"Because there's no point." I put my hand over her phone to prevent her from dialing the rest of the number.

"Whatever Donte, you know if this happened to you or some dude disrespected you the way she did me you would've been mad as hell and ready to whoop some ass."

"Yeah I agree, but ain't no point of calling and arguing with her just let me handle it." After a brief silence Niki agreed. "Okay but if you don't handle it I will."

The next day Layla set up an appointment for us to meet her around twelve to check out flower arrangements for the wedding. Niki had some work to handle at the law firm last minute so I agreed to meet Layla in her place. When I arrived at the flower shop Layla was already there.

"Hey, what are you doing here? I thought Niki was supposed to meet me?" Layla asked with a huge grin on her face.

"She had something come up last minute and couldn't make it so I agreed to meet you instead."

"Oh well I'm glad you're here." Layla said and attempted to hug me. Kindly stepping back to avoid her hug I looked at her as if she were crazy and headed over towards the counter leaving her standing by the door. Slightly embarrassed, Layla adjusted her outfit and walked over to join me at the counter.

"Good afternoon, I'm Mary. How may I help you today?" The florist behind the counter asked with a smile. "We had an appointment to look at some flower arrangements." Layla replied.

"What's the occasion, a wedding?"

"Yes ma'am," Layla said with a smile.

"Oh sounds nice, so when's the big day?" Mary smiled.

"We're not sure yet we're still deciding, but we wanna go ahead and get some things done." I smiled.

"So do you have an idea what type of flowers you'd like?"

"No not really."

"Ok, let me show you what we have." After looking at various flower arrangements, I took a picture the ones I liked and sent them to Niki's phone.

"So have you made a decision?" Mary asked walking back over to the counter.

"No I think I'm gonna leave it up to my fiancé."

"Okay. Well, have you decided on anything?" Mary said turning to Layla.

"Oh no, she's not my fiancé. She's one of our wedding planners."

"Oh I'm sorry, I didn't know," Mary apologized.

"It's fine. I'll have my fiancé come by to make the final decision."

"Okay, here's my card just have her ask for me when she comes." Mary smiled handing me her card.

"Okay, thank you Mary, I'll do that."

Layla ran to catch up to me as I headed for the door. "So

you wanna go get something to eat, maybe we can go over the wedding plans?" Layla smiled brightly.

"Nah I'm good, I got some things to do."

"We don't have to stay that long. I know a great restaurant right up the street. It's literally within walking distance."

"Look, I said no." I began to get irritated from Layla following behind me.

"Will you hold up for a minute?" Layla grabbed my arm to stop me from walking.

"What do you want from me Layla, really?"

"Honestly I think you're a handsome man and I'd like to get to know you a little better. I know you got a fiancé and all, but she doesn't have to know anything I can keep my mouth shut."

I stared at her with my face twisted up. "Bitch are you crazy? I'm about to get married. Do you really think I'd risk that to mess around with you?" I laughed lightly as if she were a joke. "Damn Niki said you was on some scandalous shit and she was right."

"I just thought that maybe..."

"You just thought what?" Annoyed, I cut her off. "What? Did you think you looked that good that I would dump my fiancé for you? You hoes are unbelievable, it amazes me how y'all think every man gone want y'all just because you got a nice ass and pretty face. That shit comes a dime a dozen so you ain't shit special." I laughed. "Even if I wasn't engaged I still wouldn't fuck wit you. I don't date scandalous hoes." I turned to walk away then stopped in my tracks. "Aye as a matter of fact, I don't want you working with us no more and I'm a let Cynthia know that first thing tomorrow morning." Dismissing her, I continued to my car. Surprised and embarrassed by my reaction, she couldn't do anything but stand in the middle of the sidewalk and watch me drive away.

"Hey baby how'd everything go?" Niki asked as I entered the house.

"Alright I guess. I thought you were gonna meet me at the flower shop after you finished up your work."

"I was but by time I got done it was too late. So what happened with Layla? Was everything cool?"

"You was right about her. She tried to ask me out talking 'bout you ain't gotta know nothing."

Niki got angry and started yelling. "I told you she was trying to be slick! I knew she was up to something! I can't stand hoes!"

"Don't trip. I called Cynthia and left her a message that we all need to meet up to talk. I should be getting a call back soon."

"Good cuz I want her ass fired," Niki said heading to the kitchen to grab something to drink.

"Damn." I massaged my temples.

"What wrong baby?" Niki asked me with a concerned tone as she sipped on her juice.

"I forgot to call Mason. We were supposed to go pick out our tuxes today. What time is it?" I asked Niki looking around for my cell phone.

"It's going on 1:45." Niki replied.

Shit, the game starts around two o'clock at least we can make that I hope. I quickly dialed Mason's number.

"Hello." Mason answered picking up on the third ring.

"Hey man, I forgot we were supposed to check out tuxes this morning. I got caught up handling some stuff for Niki."

"You good man, I had to go to a last minute doctor's appointment with Char so I couldn't make it no way. We still on for basketball?" Mason asked.

"Yeah I'm throwing my stuff on now. We might be a little late but we should be alright."

"We good them fools never start on time no way." Mason laughed.

"Alright I'll be there in 15 minutes." I grabbed my jacket, pecked Niki on the lips, and rushed out the door.

We finally made it to the gym and after all that rushing like Mason predicted, them fools hadn't even started yet. "Y'all just in time to get in on the bet." Tyrone said as he greeted me and Mason at the door.

"How much we going for?" I asked as I threw my gym bag on a bench nearby.

"No more than fifty dollars, everybody waiting on payday."

"That's cool we in." I grabbed a basketball and ran out on the court. After playing two games most of the guys were ready to quit.

"Damn y'all already tired?" Mason said still full of energy.

"Yeah man, I got a few things I gotta handle for the wife this evening," one of the players said.

"That's cool, so when we meeting up again?"

"This weekend if y'all want to," Tyrone replied.

"Alright, I'll call and let you know if we can make it or not." Mason and I gave Tyrone dap. As everyone gathered their things a loud commotion was heard from outside the gym.

"Aye, y'all hear that?" Tyrone asked listening intently.

"Yeah man, it sounds like somebody arguing." Mason said looking towards the entrance. "Let's go check it out." As we walked outside to check out the commotion a dude in a ski mask ran up and pointed his gun at Mason. "Remember me muthafucka!" He snatched his ski mask off his head, let off two shots, and took off running. "Mason!" I attempted to catch him before he hit the ground but it was as if everything was in fast forward. With empty arms outstretched I looked down to find Mason on the ground with blood gushing from his wounds. "Get that muthafucka!" I yelled as a few of the guys took off after the shooter. "Mason man talk to me." I applied pressure to his wounds with his shirt to slow down the bleeding. My free hand was covered in blood as I frantically fumbled around in my gym bag looking for my cell phone.

"Is he responding?" Tyrone asked running over to me.

"Nah man, call 911." As Tyrone did as he was asked, I continued to talk to Mason and apply pressure to his wounds. "Hold on man somebody's coming. Keep breathing." I kept telling him when I noticed he was starting to close his eyes. Tyrone came over and looked at Mason to tell the operator his condition. "Is somebody on the way?" I asked Tyrone beginning to get impatient.

"Yeah, she said keep applying pressure to his wound and try to keep him awake."

"I'm trying man, I'm trying." I told Tyrone trying to stay focused. "Stay up Mason you gotta be here for Char and your kids. You gonna be alright just hang in there." Tears welled up in my eyes unwillingly. I tried to sniff them back but after a while, the dam broke, making it hard to see through blurry eyes.

Chapter 11

Candy

It's been two weeks since I started working at Club Paradise and I've made way more money than I ever made back in St. Louis. These guys out here ain't cheap, with the money they tipping I'll have my own place in no time. Today, like every other day, I found an outfit to put on and prepared myself to head out on stage. I was fixing my wig and finishing my makeup when I heard my name called to appear on stage. Here we go. When the music began to play I slowly danced my way on stage. Stopping right next to the stripper pole I dropped down into a split and lifted myself up off the floor with the pole as I twisted my body to do an upside down split. Bringing my legs down to the side, I twirled around the pole and eased myself on the floor. As I danced erotically to the beat of the music I ripped my shirt off, exposing a bikini top that left little to the imagination, then tossed it at one of the men sitting in front of the stage. As I slowly danced to the end of the stage I noticed a face that looked quite familiar to me.

Attempting to get a closer look, I eased down off the stage and began to toy with the men in the crowd hoping to make it over to Mr. Familiar before my song ended. The closer I got the more I was held up by men grabbing my hand and trying to feel me up as I danced. I finally made it over to his table, but the song ended so I had to head back on stage. Dammit, I was almost there. I was disappointed as I walked backstage. Hopefully he'd still be there when I made my rounds for lap dances. If it's who I think it is he's gonna be in a world of trouble. I quickly changed outfits and headed back out front to sneak a peek. I knew it, that's Tia's husband. I know he ain't taking that stripper in the backroom! Oooh I'm telling Tia. I continued to follow them without being noticed.

"Hey baby can I get a lap dance?" A male voice said from behind me as he grabbed my hand.

"Huh?" I pulled away from him.

"A lap dance, do you do those?"

"Yeah I'm sorry." I turned to face him.

"Wait a minute, aren't you that jazz musician, Taye Hicks? I've seen your name all over the place. I love your music," I smiled.

"Thank you, I'm surprised you know me."

"Why is that?" I looked at him curious.

"It's not every day that I have strippers tell me they like my music."

"Just because I'm a stripper it doesn't mean I can't like jazz."

"I didn't mean to offend you. I'm just saying that it doesn't happen often." Taye attempted to redeem himself. "Anyway, how about that lap dance?"

"Sure whatever you want," I said dryly as Taye stuffed a $50 in my thong. As I slowly grinded on his lap Taye began to hold my waist, pulling me in closer to him.

"Yeah I like that keep doing what you doing." Taye began to grind with me. "What you doing when you get out of here?"

"Going home." I rolled my eyes irritated.

"If you this good here I wonder how you are in bed. I wanna find out. Why don't you come over my way when you get off work, I'll pay you."

"Naw I'm good." I waved him off.

"How much you want? I got plenty of money, name your price."

"This session is over." I abruptly got up off his lap.

"What's wrong with you? That's what you do ain't it, fuck for money?"

Offended by his statement I crossed my arms and glared at him. "No that's not what I do! I dance for money, I'm not a prostitute!"

"Y'all taking men in back rooms and shit, sleeping with them so how am I supposed to know?"

"All of us don't do that!"

"Have you done it before?" Taye asked me confused.

"Yeah."

"Well what's the problem then? I said I'd pay you."

"Look I don't want your damn money, just because I'm a stripper it doesn't mean I don't have feelings or that I shouldn't be treated with some kind of respect! True enough I do this for a living, but this job isn't who I am. There's more to me than just this job! I sleep with who I want to sleep with. I'm not a hoe and I don't have a pimp which means I choose to do what I want to do and I won't stand here and be degraded by you!"

"Honestly you don't need my help with that you do that on your own every day you step foot in this job. Look what you do for a living." Taye smirked at me. "As a matter of fact, here take some money obviously you're desperate for it. Have a good night." Taye tossed a hundred dollar bill at me and walked off. Feeling like cheap trash, I picked the money up off the floor and headed backstage to change clothes and go home for the night. I've never felt so cheap in my life. I know people don't look at me like nothing nice because of my job, but I've never been degraded the way I have tonight. I choked back tears at the thought of what had just happened. As I headed to my car, I noticed my cousin Tia's car in the parking lot. My curiosity got the best of me so I walked over to the car and peeked through the window. "Oh my God!" The stripper lifted her head out of Thomas lap when she heard me yelling. "So is this what you do with your spare time when you're not with my cousin?" Thomas stared at me in shock. "Get out of my cousin's car!" I yanked the stripper out of the car by her hair.

"Wait a minute you don't understand!" Thomas pled.

"There's nothing to understand. Either you tell Tia or I will!"

"She doesn't have to know about this. What can I give you to keep you quiet?" Thomas followed me around the car.

"Nothing. Here she is thinking she got something special, but you're no better than the other men she's dated, actually you're worse!" I shook my head.

"It's just that I can't get Tia to do the things I want her to do. She's so old fashioned! I've tried to understand her logic and deal with it but I can't, Tia would never perform oral sex on me and swallow my…"

"That's enough I really don't need or want to hear that." I was disgusted.

"But she should want to do these things to please me."

"I don't care Thomas. That still doesn't give you the right to cheat on her! If she's not giving you what you want and you're not happy then leave!"

"Please don't tell her!" Thomas begged as he followed me to my newly leased car.

"I'm a tell you like this, you got two days to come clean and if you don't I'm telling her everything." I slammed my car door leaving Thomas standing in the middle of the parking lot with his boxers on. The next day I got up early hoping to avoid him, but low and behold the moment I stepped into the hallway I ran right into him. "So you tell her yet?" I folded my arms across my chest.

"No not yet, I'm gonna tell her when she gets home from work tonight." Thomas stared at the floor to avoid eye contact.

"I hope so cuz today's your last day to come clean. If you haven't told her by tomorrow I'm gonna talk to her."

"Yes I know you've made that very clear."

"I hope so." I bumped pass him and headed down the hall. That clown got another thing coming if he thinks I'm letting him get away with that mess, blood is thicker than water and I ain't letting my cousin get played for a fool.

I had to be at work soon so I dropped SJ off at daycare and headed in. No matter what time of day it is the club is always packed. I've never seen a strip club where the men never go home. It's as if they have no lives or wives. The moment I stepped my foot in the door my manager, Rudy, wanted me to go on stage. Supposedly, Lisa, one of the strippers, called in sick and couldn't make it in. Since I'm the designated replacement, they're rushing me to go on stage next. See, I have no problem covering for people, but I would at least like to chill for a minute to get myself mentally prepared.

I quickly rushed backstage, threw on an outfit, and waited for them to call my name. As soon as they did, I danced my way to the pole in the middle of the stage and noticed none other than Taye Hicks sitting in the front row taking a sip of his drink. Slightly rolling my eyes, I took a deep breath and continued to move my body to the beat of the music. I shook and gyrated on and in front of every man but him. I peeked over and laughed at the look of envy and lust that appeared across his face. Taye gestured for me to come over by waving his money in the air like a flag, but I continued to ignore him as if he wasn't there. Once my dance was over I looked over at him and we happened to lock eyes so I kindly smiled and headed backstage. Laughing to myself about our encounter, I changed into my next outfit and headed out front to give a few lap dances. As I went from table to table, I felt someone grab my hand.

"I guess my money ain't good enough for you huh?" Taye said as he stood behind me.

"No it's not."

Rubbing his hand across his face Taye stared at me and smiled slightly. "Let me talk to you for a minute, can you get off the floor?"

"Maybe, but why should I?" I gave him much attitude.

"Look man kill the attitude. I just need to talk to you for a minute and then you can get back to your lap dances."

"There you go with the insults again." I rolled my eyes.

"Can you do it or not?" Taye looked at me frustrated.

After a short pause, I sighed. "Fine, step over here." I lead him into the hallway. "So what do you want?"

"I wanted to apologize to you for the way I came at you the other day, I wasn't trying to offend you. So to make it up to you. I want to take you out."

"What? You wanna take out a stripper?" I laughed sarcastically with my arms folded.

"Well here go my number, call me when you're done being childish." Taye handed me his card and abruptly walked off. He is such a smart ass. I blew out a breath and stuffed his number in my top.

After finishing up a long day of work, I gathered my things and headed for the parking lot to get in my car. I felt someone following behind me as I walked briskly to my car so I turned around and ended up face to face with Thomas. "Why are you following me, you trying to kidnap me or something?"

"No, I just wanted to talk to you. I called you a couple times, but you kept walking." Thomas was now walking along side me.

"What you need to talk about?"

"Tia, have you talked to her yet?" Thomas asked staring at me.

"No. You were supposed to talk to her, but I take it as you didn't."

"I couldn't, I didn't want to hurt her."

"Well you should've thought about that before you did

what you did."

"I know but what's done is done and it won't happen again so there's no point of you telling her."

"It doesn't work like that Thomas. I'm not gonna stand by and watch you lie to her. I'm telling her whether you want me to or not."

"It's like you want to see her hurt. Seeing how you're her cousin you shouldn't want to see her upset." Thomas said to me with a desperate look on his face.

"No, I don't want to see her hurt but she needs to know."

"What can I give you to keep silent?" Thomas asked with a sadistic look in his eye as he grabbed my arm.

"Nothing, you can't buy me out of my decision." I looked at him like he was crazy and attempted to jerk my arm away.

"I'm not gonna let you mess up my relationship. Everything was fine until you got here! Now you wanna come and mess everything up but I'm not gonna let that happen!" Thomas held my arm even tighter.

"You don't have a choice now let me go!" I tried to pry his hand off my arm, but his grip only got tighter. Starting to panic, I yelled for help and continued to try to pull away.

"Either you keep your mouth shut or I'll make your life a living hell!" Thomas squeezed my arm tighter.

"Let her go!" Someone yelled from across the parking lot. I peered across the parking lot and saw Taye running towards us. "Get off her!" Taye grabbed Thomas and put him in a chokehold.

"Alright, alright!" Thomas said struggling to breathe as he threw his hands up in submission. Taye finally let Thomas go and pushed him causing him to stumble to the ground. "If I see you again I'm gonna do more than choke you. Now get the fuck outta here!"

Thomas picked himself up off the ground and dusted himself off. "You heard what I said Candy," he warned before walking off.

As we watched Thomas get in his car and speed off I shook my head.

"You alright?" Taye asked noticing I looked a bit shaken.

"Yeah I'm good, that was just my cousin's fool ass husband. He's mad because I caught him cheating on her and threatened to tell her. Thank you for helping me out. I didn't think he'd act like that."

"It's cool, I got you." Taye smiled.

"So what you 'bout to do?"

"Nothing, go home."

"You wanna go grab something to eat?"

"Yeah, I guess I ain't doing nothing else." I smiled. "So where you wanna go?"

"Don't worry 'bout it I'll surprise you. Just follow me." Taye said as he headed to his car.

Twenty minutes later we arrived at a small yet cute diner called Gloria's Country Kitchen. "Is this it? I've never been here." I admired the place as I got out my car.

"Yep, this is my Aunt Gloria's diner. It's been here for about thirty years and it's always packed with business." Taye replied proudly with a bright smile. "Come on I'll introduce you to my Aunt." As we walked in a slim brown-skinned woman in an apron walked up, kissed Taye on the cheek, and gave him a big hug.

"Hey, what you doing here? I thought you weren't coming in town until tomorrow?" The woman questioned Taye with a smile.

"That was the plan, but I was able to change my flight to get here earlier."

"Great, so who's your lady friend here?"

"This is Candy, Candy this is my Aunt Gloria." Taye introduced us.

"Nice to meet you honey." Gloria said with a thick southern accent as she gave me a motherly hug.

"I hope you two are hungry because I added some new items to the menu I need you to try out." Gloria escorted Taye and I to a table and a few minutes later brought out two glasses of juice and appetizers. "These are a couple of the appetizers I added to the menu for the breakfast lovers, homemade French toast sticks topped with strawberries and sprinkled with powdered sugar and stuffed hash browns. I hope y'all like it, eat up." Gloria smiled then headed back to the kitchen.

"Oh my God, everything smells and looks so good. I really like the hash browns they're so crunchy. I've never seen hash browns shaped like cheese balls." I stuffed my mouth with another one.

"Yeah my aunt likes to be different, she prides herself on originality." Taye responded while dipping his French toast stick in a cup of syrup. "So why haven't I seen you in the strip club before? I know most of the dancers that work there, but the other day was my first time seeing you."

"I just moved here about two weeks ago and my cousin Tia knows the manager so she got me a job there."

"Why would she get you a job at a strip club she couldn't find you nothing better?"

"Yeah, but I figured it would be easier to find a job stripping since I already had experience. Most jobs nowadays want too much, every time you turn around they're asking for more stuff. Like at first all you needed was a high school diploma but now they want you to have a Bachelor's or Master's degree, which I don't have, so why bother." I took a sip of my apple juice. "So why are you always there? Your girl works there or something?"

"Naw my uncle owns the club. I just come around to help out every now and then when I'm in town. How does your cousin know the manager, does she strip too?"

"No, she knows him from school. They took classes in college together."

"Oh, so you staying with her while you're out here?"

"Yes until I find a place of my own. Where do you live?"

"In Long Beach, California." Taye smiled.

"Now that's nice. How long have you lived there?"

"About ten years. I'm thinking about moving back here though."

"Why? With all those palm trees and beaches around every day out there probably feels like a vacation."

"Yeah but I can see the same thing here."

"Yeah that's true, but I'd love to live out there." I smiled excited at the thought.

"Don't get me wrong, it's nice living there but all my family and friends are out here. I miss being here especially around the holidays."

"That's understandable." I watched Gloria sit two large

plates of food on the table and walk away. "So, you got any wives, kids, or girlfriends?" I smiled.

"No I don't. I was married once but my wife passed away from breast cancer and I've been single ever since."

"I'm so sorry, I didn't mean to pry." I felt bad for asking and couldn't look at him so I looked down at the table instead.

"It's cool, it's been a few years so it's easier to talk about it…so you got any kids, husbands, or boyfriends?" Taye asked me attempting to lighten the mood.

"No husbands or boyfriends but I do have a son. He'll be three in about a month." I smiled.

"I ain't trying to be nosy but where's his father?"

"He's in prison," I replied avoiding eye contact with Taye.

"Prison? So much for the father-son relationship. I know that's got to be hard on you raising him by yourself. Especially having to explain why his daddy's not around. What did he do?"

"It's a long story." I wasn't interested in going into detail.

"We got time unless you planning on heading out early."

I sat nervously for a minute. After a long pause, I decided to go ahead and tell Taye about Shawn and how he ended up in jail.

"Long story short, he had me attacked and tried to make me lose SJ because I refused to abort him. I ended up in the hospital for a minute but afterwards I pressed charges against him. The Judge ended up giving him five years in prison then tacked on two more after he assaulted a couple of the officers when they tried to carry him out of court.

Taye looked confused. "So you mean to tell me you still talk to this fool even though he tried to kill you and your son?"

"Yes. Forgiveness is a hard thing, but I had to do it for the sake of my son. I didn't want him to grow up not knowing who his father is, plus Shawn has changed a lot since SJ's been born. He's actually trying to be a good father."

"How good of a father can he really be in jail? He shouldn't even want his son seeing him in there. I know I wouldn't." Taye looked upset by the situation.

I attempted to defend my position. "He didn't want me bringing him up there at first but I chose to do it anyway. I figured SJ needed to meet his father. And maybe seeing him living in the condition he's living in, he wouldn't want to grow up and end up like him."

"Yeah, I guess that's one way you can look at it. So considering you have a son and all stripping probably isn't the best profession for you, wouldn't you agree?" Taye looked at me.

"Yeah I can agree with that, but it pays the bills."

"Why don't you go to school or something?" Taye suggested.

"School takes too long, I need money now."

"Alright then let's make a deal. If I can find you something that'll pay you a decent amount of money where you won't have to strip anymore will you take it?"

"I don't know it depends on what it is. What, you got something lined up for me?" I asked him hopefully.

"Maybe let me see what I can do." Taye said as he ate a fork full of lasagna.

Chapter 12

Donte

As I rode in the back of the ambulance with Mason, all I could think about was getting revenge. "He's gonna pay for what he did to you I promise you that," I whispered to Mason as tears welled up in my eyes. When we finally made it to the hospital, the EMTs rushed Mason inside. After filling out a few forms for Mason I called Niki and had her to call Charlene. Noticing the look of defeat on my face the nurse at the front desk patted my hand and said, "Don't worry sir your friend is in good hands I promise you." She had hoped her reassurance would provide me with some type of comfort. I gave a forced smile then stood by watching in silence.

A half an hour later Charlene and Niki came rushing through the doors. A panicked Charlene asked snapping me out of my trance. "Where's Mason?" I turned to face her and watched as tears streamed down her face. Attempting to maintain my composure, I stood up. "They took him to the back." I said gesturing for them to sit down. "I haven't heard anything yet but

I'm sure he's gonna be fine. He's a fighter and he has a lot to live for so I'm sure he'll be alright." I said trying to believe my own words. As we all sat in the waiting room anticipating what we hoped would be good news, I explained what happened to Mason in further detail.

"So you know who did this?" Charlene asked me visibly upset.

"Yeah, it was this dude named Trevon that we got into it with during a game a couple years back. Dude got mad cuz he had to pay out two hundred dollars on a bet he got in on. Last minute he tried to renege and got silly so him and Mason ended up fighting."

"I think Mason told me about him." Charlene scratched her head trying to jog her memory. "Have you told the police about him?"

"Naw I haven't had a chance to. We got here right before y'all did."

"We can call them now." Charlene said to me while pulling out her cell phone.

"Don't worry about it. Tyrone and some of the other guys that were there when it happened are already taking care of it. They were talking to the police when we left."

"Just try to relax Char, I know it's hard but I'm sure we'll find out something soon," Niki said trying to calm her.

Two hours later a doctor walked out into the waiting area and asked if we were Mason Clark's family, Charlene stood up awaiting the doctor's next words. "I'm Doctor Stein. I worked on your husband." He said as he shook all of our hands. "I have good news. Your husband's going to be just fine." Charlene let out a sigh of relief and for the first time in hours we were all able to smile. "Two of the bullets that hit him were lodged into his abdomen pretty deep so it was a bit difficult to remove them but with a lot of time and patience we were able to get them."

"Oh thank you doctor, thank you so much." Charlene let out a breath of air as tears welled up in her eyes.

"That's what we're here for to save lives." The doctor smiled. "I must tell you though your husband is a lucky man, a few more inches over to the right, the bullet would've hit his liver and it would've been fatal so consider this a blessing?" He paused slightly. "I do have to tell you one of the bullets wounded his leg pretty badly so he'll be in a wheelchair for a while but with some consistent physical therapy he'll be as good as new."

"Oh thank God! I'm just happy he's alive." Charlene and Niki embraced.

"So when will we be able to see him?" I asked relieved.

"He's still out of it right now from the medicine we've given him but you're free to go sit with him if you like."

"That would be great Doctor Stein thank you so much." Charlene said happy to hear the news.

"It's my pleasure. Just follow me and I'll take you to his room."

After entering Mason's room, Charlene walked over to his bedside and kissed him on his forehead with tear-filled eyes. "Thank God you're okay." She whispered in his ear as she rubbed her belly. "Our son's gonna need his father. I can't raise him to be a man without you baby. We need you." She leaned over the bed rail and hugged him around his neck.

After a few hours Charlene told Niki and I to go home and

get some rest. "I'll stay with him. If he wakes up I'll give you guys a call."

Niki and I gathered our things and gave Mason one last look before leaving. "Get some rest Charlene you need to stay well rested for the baby."

"I will." She replied giving us a half smile.

Chapter 13

Niki

After leaving the hospital, it was hard for Donte and I to relax. We decided to grab a bite to eat and walk around Laclede's Landing by The Arch, to get some fresh air. As we searched for a spot to eat, my phone began ringing.

"Hi Niki, this is Cynthia. I got your voicemail and wanted to see when you want to meet up."

"Today if at all possible."

"It's almost 6:30 now so if it'll work for you I can meet you around 7:00 or 7:30."

"I'm at Laclede's Landing by The Arch. Can you meet me here by 7:30?"

"Sure, that's fine. I'll see you at 7:30."

"Who was that?" Donte asked me curiously.

"Cynthia, she wants to meet up so we can talk."

"That's good. I hope y'all can work things out."

"Me too."

No sooner than we finished our meal, Cynthia called me

and said she was by The Arch. We quickly finished our drinks, paid for our food, and headed over to meet her. As we approached, I saw Cynthia sitting on a bench talking to Layla. Trying to remain calm, I walked over with Donte in toe and greeted them both. Cynthia scooted over to offer us a seat then we quickly got into discussion. "So how are things going Niki?" Cynthia smiled.

"Pretty good, but I'm interested in making a few changes in the wedding planning."

"Are you unhappy with our services?" Cynthia asked with a look of concern.

"Not on your end but with Layla yes."

"What's the problem?"

"Honestly I no longer want Layla assisting with our wedding."

"Excuse me!" Layla interjected. "What is that supposed to mean?"

"It means that I only want to work with Cynthia and not you." Layla and I glared at each other.

"Did you not understand that I would be assisting with the wedding when you signed the contract?"

"Oh that was perfectly understood, but it was also understood that if I wasn't happy with the services the contract wouldn't be binding."

"Well unfortunately I'm Cynthia's only assistant so you have no choice but to work with me."

"Well how about this, your services are no longer needed."

"What?" Layla looked at me confused. "You're fired." Leaving Layla to digest the news, I stood up to leave. "Are you really gonna be that petty, why are you being so childish?"

"Excuse me? You trying to come on to my fiancé is extremely unprofessional, tacky, and inexcusable so don't lecture me about being childish when it's your behavior that's pushed me to this point."

"Honey I don't want your man, if I did believe me I could have him."

"I guess that's why you were practically throwing yourself on him at the flower shop." I smirked.

"No honey your man came at me. So you need to be trying to check him not me."

Donte walked over and gently moved me to the side. "Cynthia, can we talk for a minute?" Surprised to hear Donte speak up, I looked on as Cynthia and Donte walked off to chat. I refused to say another word to Layla so I moved over a couple of benches and waited for Donte and Cynthia to return. About five minutes later, they walked back over.

"Okay, Donte gave me all the details of what happened at the flower shop. I apologize for Layla's blatant lack of respect and professionalism. I can assure you that as long as I've been in this business I have never had a situation like this. I am very disappointed and embarrassed about this and I would like to figure out a way to retain your business. The last thing I want is for the two of you to discontinue our services due to a bad encounter. Considering this, I will only charge you half price for the entire wedding and I'll provide both you and Donte with a suite at the hotel the day of the wedding free of charge." I looked at Donte and contemplated her offer for a minute.

"What about Layla, will she still be assisting with our wedding?"

"Unfortunately it's too late to find a replacement so yes. But what I can do is meet the two of you myself for any other appointments you have set. That way there won't be any other issues or conflicts." After a brief silence, Donte and I accepted Cynthia's offer and agreed to meet her the next day to sign off on the new terms of agreement.

After our meeting with Cynthia, we checked in with Charlene to see if Mason's condition had improved. "How's Mason?" I asked hoping for good news.

"He's still out of it, the doctor said we're just gonna have to wait it out."

"Well we're gonna head up there to keep you company."

"No go ahead and go home to get some rest, I'll be fine. I'll just call you if anything changes."

"Are you sure Char we're not that far away we can be up there within the next twenty minutes?"

"No it's fine. Go on home I promise I'll be alright, just come by in the morning." As much as I tried to talk my friend into allowing us to come and keep her company she refused and was adamant about us going home. The last thing we wanted to do was cause her any more stress so we did as she asked and agreed to come back in the morning

"Alright we'll see you in the morning, make sure you get some rest Char. You're not gonna be any good to anyone if you're up stressing all night, especially those twins."

"I know I'll probably try to doze off once we get off the phone, thank you for checking on us."

"Char you're like my sister and Mason's like a brother to Donte so of course we're gonna be here for you."

119

"Thanks Niki."

"No thanks needed just get some rest."

After hanging up with Charlene, Donte and I went home to get some rest. But as much as I wanted to go to sleep, I couldn't. All I could do was toss and turn until eventually I got annoyed and went downstairs to watch some TV. An hour passed and I still couldn't sleep so I continued to hang out on the living room couch.

"Baby why aren't you in bed." Donte asked me as he came down the stairs.

"I couldn't sleep."

"Well you can't stay down here all night we gotta get up in the morning. I was hoping we could grab some breakfast before we go to the hospital."

"I know. I just can't sleep with all this going on. I hate seeing Charlene and Mason going through this."

"I know and I hate that this happened to, but you got to get some rest baby."

"I don't know Donte I'm not good at counting sheep and I don't want to keep you up all night."

"Well come upstairs, I'm sure I can find a way to put you to sleep."

"How?"

"You know how." He replied giving me a devilish grin.

"You are so bad."

"I know now come to bed." Donte walked over, pulled me off the couch, and escorted me upstairs. I stared at Donte as he got in the bed. Then he gently took both of my hands and pulled me down to him.

"It's okay baby everything is gonna be fine."

"Mason will be back to normal in no time and Charlene's gonna have a set of healthy newborn twins."

"Is that what you keep telling yourself?"

"No, that's what I know." Donte said as he lifted my chin to look up at him.

"Now lay down with me so you can rest." I snuggled underneath Donte's arm and within twenty minutes I was fast asleep.

Chapter 14

Ariel

Mason finally came back home, but things were strange for a while. It felt like we were more like roommates than a married couple. He rarely talked to me, came in and out the house whenever he felt like it, and refused to stay in the same room with me. I grew tired of being treated that way, but I figured if I hung in there things would eventually change. Sure enough, after a couple months went by of me doing the right thing, Mason began to warm up to me again. He began to come home regularly and talk a little more. Things were still slightly uncomfortable, but slowly he was coming around. Now even though things had gotten better at home I just couldn't seem to get Keith off my mind. There was something about this guy that piqued my interests. Whenever I could get away we'd meet up and spend time together. Everything between Keith and I had been great until this one day, which had to be the worst day of my life. I went over his house to chill for a while and we started messing around. "I love the way you feel," he said as he passionately kissed me. Things began to get pretty hot and heavy between us until Keith heard someone pull up in the driveway. Interested in who it could be, he told me to hold on a minute.

"What's wrong?" I asked, noticing he was acting a bit strange.

"Nothing I thought I heard someone outside," he said as he scanned the driveway. "Oh shit!" I heard Keith say under his breath.

"Keith are you okay?"

"Yeah, I need you to do me a favor baby."

"What's that?" I looked at him confused.

"Can we do this another day?"

"Another day, why?"

"I forgot one of my clients was coming over tonight. I thought it was supposed to be tomorrow night." I watched as he nervously fidgeted with his pants.

"Keith!" I heard a woman yell from downstairs.

"A client huh? I don't know many business men who give their clients keys to their house."

"I can't really explain right now." Keith said to me as he scrambled around the room looking for clothes to throw on.

"Keith!" The woman yelled again.

"Keith who is that? And don't lie to me or I won't leave." I stared at him.

"It's my wife! I'm married."

"You're what! Why didn't you tell me this from the beginning? I told you the truth so it would've been nice if you had done the same."

"Look I'm sorry, I didn't mean to lie to you. I promise

we'll talk about this later I just can't talk right now. Please work with me on this one, I swear I'll make this up to you." Keith said practically begging me to leave. After a brief pause, I finally agreed.

"Alright fine. I'll leave, but we seriously need to talk." I quickly threw my clothes on and waited on him to decide what to do next. "I'll be right back just stay here." Keith darted out of the bedroom as I shook my head in disbelief.

Listening intently through the door, I could hear Keith ask his wife, Jacqueline, why she was home so early. She explained that her trip ended sooner than planned so she decided to surprise him by coming home early to spend a little time with him. Jacqueline hugged Keith. Keith was still slightly aroused from messing around but he hoped Jacqueline wouldn't notice.

"Oh you really must've missed me." She said glancing down at his pants. "We'll handle that later." She smiled slightly. "So what took you so long to answer me? I called you like four times."

"I was in the bathroom. I couldn't just hop off the toilet." Keith nervously shifted his weight from one leg to the other.

"Well let me put my stuff down so I can tell you about my trip." Jacqueline began to walk towards the bedroom but Keith grabbed her hand.

"Jackie baby why don't you sit down and relax. You've been on the road all day. Let me get your luggage for you."

"No it's okay. I can do it. I had plenty of rest on the airplane so I'm fully energized." Keith's heart began to beat wildly and beads of sweat formed on his forehead as they entered the bedroom.

"You sure you got it baby? I don't mind getting that for you."

"Keith I'm fine, why you acting so funny?"

"I'm not I just missed you and don't want you doing too much since you just got in. I just want you to relax. I'll even cook dinner for you since I haven't done it in a while."

"That's sweet baby." Jacqueline kissed Keith on the lips and hugged him tightly. "Alright since you insist, I'll go relax downstairs and let you take care of my suitcases. Thank you baby."

I quickly grabbed my keys and purse the moment they left the room and headed for the door. Keith startled me when he burst through the door with suitcases in his hand. "I'm sorry about all of this baby." He attempted to hug and kiss me on the cheek but I pulled away so he stepped back to give me my space.

"So where were you hiding?"

"In the bathroom, anyway how am I supposed to get out of here?"

"She's in the living room right now. I'm gonna run her a bath to occupy her. When she gets in the tub I'm gonna let you out through the back door."

"You make me feel like some teenage girl you snuck in your house while your parents were sleep." I rolled my eyes.

"If I let you out the front door it's a chance she'll hear you."

"Fine just let me know when you're ready." I folded my arms, plopped back down on the bed, and sucked my teeth as Keith rushed back out of the room. About an hour later Keith came back in the room. "Sorry it took so long I had to make sure she was straight so she wouldn't call me for a while. You got everything?"

"Yeah I'm good. Let's go." I said as I followed him down

the stairs. "Are you sure she's not gonna hear us?"

"Yeah, I'm positive. She's using the bathroom in the master bedroom on the first floor."

"How many rooms do you have?"

"Six bedrooms and three and a half baths." Keith answered as he walked with me out the back door and to my car. "Are you going to be okay heading home?"

"Yeah I'm good." I gave Keith a weak smile.

"Alright call me so I'll know you made it okay." Keith tried to kiss me on the cheek but I turned my head. He stepped back and stared at me for a minute. "I'll call you when I get in, have a good night." I rode off then glimpsed up at my rearview mirror and noticed Keith still standing in the same spot watching me disappear into the night.

Deep in thought and in need of a friend I decided to call Dana to vent. She picked up after two rings. "Hey girl."

"Hey, you alright?" Dana asked noticing the tone in my voice.

I sighed. "Do you know that bastard is married?"

"Who Keith?"

"Yes."

"Dang. When did you find out?"

"Tonight, his wife popped up at the house."

"Well, you're married too so why are you mad?" Dana asked me confused.

"Because he lied to me. He should've told me, I told him."

"So are you gonna stop seeing him?"

"I don't know, most likely yes."

"So what happened with your problem?"

"What problem?" I awaited Dana's response confused.

"Your pregnancy problem, did you ever come on your cycle?"

"Yeah, but something was different. I can't really explain it."

"How? Have you been feeling okay?"

"Somewhat, I've just been tired more than usual."

"Did you ever take a pregnancy test?"

"No, I figured since I came on my cycle I'm not pregnant. I haven't been vomiting or craving any odd foods so I must be okay. I'm probably tired from stressing about Mason."

"Have you slept with him since he's been home?" Dana asked me.

"Yes, especially lately."

"Knowing you've been sleeping with Keith unprotected? Do you know how often this dude gets checkups? Keith could have anything, the last thing you want is to bring something home to Mason and have to explain where it came from." Dana was surprised at my lack of safety precautions.

"Dana I don't need a lecture. I just wanted someone to talk to."

"I'm not trying to lecture you, but if you're pregnant would you even know who the father is?"

"It doesn't matter cuz even if it is Keith's I'll still tell Mason it's his, I'm not gonna let that ruin my marriage."

"That's wrong Ariel! You can't have Mason thinking that's his kid when it's not. That's not fair to him. Mason's a good dude and he doesn't deserve that."

"Why are you getting so defensive? It's not like it's gonna

affect you in any way." I exhaled annoyed at Dana's lack of loyalty. The last time I checked she was *my* friend not Mason's.

"Look I gotta go Ariel. I'll call you tomorrow." Then I heard a click.

"Hello, Dana?" I called through my earpiece as I pulled into my driveway but all I got was a dial tone. *I don't know why she's catching feelings it's not like I'm sleeping with her man.* Completely over my conversation with Dana, I got out of the car and headed in the house. I noticed Mason was still out playing basketball with Donte so I took advantage of the alone time and decided to take a nice hot bubble bath. After bathing, I put on some sweats and a tank top then got comfortable on the living room sofa. As I flipped through TV channels searching for a good movie to watch, my phone rang. "Hello?"

"Hey baby, you make it home safely?" Keith quietly spoke through the phone.

"Yeah I'm good. Let me guess your wife must be around."

"Yeah she's in the bed sleep. I'm in the bathroom right now. I just wanted to apologize again for what happened. I should've told you I was married in the beginning. I didn't want you to find out this way. I just didn't think you'd continue to seeing me knowing I'm married."

"Keith please, I told you I was married the same night we met. I couldn't be mad at you if I'm married too."

"So does this mean you're not upset with me?"

"No it doesn't. You lied to me and told me you were single. If I had known you were married, it wouldn't have caught me off guard when your wife showed up. I like knowing what I'm getting myself into. I don't like surprises. How would you feel if you came over my house thinking I'm single then all of a sudden my husband shows up?"

"I get where you're coming from. I'd be mad too, but I wouldn't stop seeing you over it…"

"I don't know Keith. Just give me some time to think about this. I really want to work things out with my husband."

"Alright I'll give you that." Keith sighed.

"Let me get off the phone because my husband should be on his way home. I'll try to give you a call tomorrow."

"Alright baby, talk to you later."

After hanging up with Keith I sat back thinking about him and how I got myself into this mess. I love my husband to death but having that person on the side has always provided me that excitement that I'm missing in my marriage. Why I got married I don't know, but I thought that's what I wanted at the time. I guess I like to have my cake and eat it too.

I watched TV a little while longer then dozed off on the couch. An hour later, I felt someone slightly shaking me on my shoulder. I looked up and saw Mason staring down at me. "Hey baby, how was the basketball game? Did y'all win?" I asked as I sat up and turned off the TV.

"It was cool. Donte and I got 50 dollars each for winning one out of three games. Usually we bet more, but the guys weren't trying to pay up tonight."

"Well 50 dollars is better than nothing." I stood up and hugged Mason. He returned the hug and wrapped his arms around my waist.

"You ready to go to bed?" Mason smiled.

"You know I am."

"I got something for you?"

"For me? What is it?" I smiled.

"You'll see." He said as he grabbed my hand and escorted me upstairs. When we got upstairs, Mason threw his gym bag on the bed and pulled out a red lace negligee. "Go try this on for me. I wanna see how you look in it."

Giddy as a schoolgirl, I took the negligee from him and darted into the bathroom. A few minutes later, I sashayed into the bedroom and modeled my lingerie as if I was on a catwalk. "Come here." Mason stood up, gently grabbed my hand, and pulled me into him. "I know we've been going through some things, but I still love you and I'm willing to work on our marriage if you are." He stared in my eyes and caressed my cheek causing me to tear up from the guilt I felt from cheating on him. At that moment, I wanted so bad to come clean so we could start over the right way but I couldn't do it and risk losing him.

"I love you too Mason and I'm willing to do whatever it takes to straighten out our marriage." Mason pulled me closer, softly kissed me on the lips, then gently laid me back on the bed.

"Mason I…"

"Shhhh." Mason put his finger up to my lips. "Don't worry about it, let's just enjoy the moment." With that said, we let nature take its course.

The next morning I saw Mason off to work and then headed over to Keith's house to break off our affair. "Hey baby." Keith smiled when he opened the door and saw me.

"Hey, is your wife here?"

"No she's at work, come in." Keith kissed me on the lips then escorted me into the living room. I sat down on the sofa and

Keith went into the kitchen. "You thirsty?"

"No I'm okay, thanks."

He came back with a bottle of water and sat down next to me on the sofa. "You alright?"

"Yeah, I just think we need to talk."

He opened his bottle of water and took a swig. "Okay, what's on your mind?"

"Where was your wife all this time we've been messing around?"

"Her mother was sick so she went back home to Kansas City for a while to help her out. She wasn't supposed to be back yet, but her mother insisted that she come back since she was feeling better."

"Why didn't you go with her if her mother was sick?"

"We never really got along and the last thing I wanted to do was upset a sick woman so I stayed behind and let her handle it."

"Oh." I sat on the couch trying to figure out how to break the news that I couldn't see him anymore.

"So is that what you rode all the way over here to talk to me about?"

"Actually no..." I cleared my throat. "I came over here to tell you that I can't see you anymore. I want to make things right at home with my husband and being with you makes that difficult to do."

"Is it because you found out I'm married? I truly apologize. I should've told you."

"No Keith, it's not that. I honestly want to work on my marriage."

Keith stared at me. "Are you sure you want to do this?"

"Yes, I think this is best for both of us." Keith was quiet for a moment and then he sighed. "I understand and I guess I have no choice but to respect your decision." He moved closer to me and put his hand on my thigh. "I'm really gonna miss you."

"I'm gonna miss you too baby." We stared at each other for a moment then he gently kissed my lips.

"Keith." I weakly attempted to pull away.

"Just one last time baby. Then I promise I'll let you go." Once again, he kissed my lips and slid his hand up my skirt. I moaned.

"Just one more time." I mumbled as he laid me back on the couch and got on top of me. He was planting kisses down my stomach when we suddenly were jerked back to reality by his phone ringing.

"Aren't you gonna answer that?"

"No." He continued to kiss down to my waist.

"What if it's your wife?"

"Don't worry about that. You just lay back and let me go to work." Keith unbuttoned his pants and slid on a condom then gave me what I was now begging for. Lost in the heat of the moment we never heard the front door unlock.

Jacqueline entered the house thinking Keith wasn't home since he said he'd been called in to work last minute. Since she got off work early, she figured she'd surprise him by cleaning the house and preparing a romantic dinner for the two of them. She began to hear noises as she walked towards the living room. "What the hell?" She said to herself staring in disbelief as Keith pumped harder inside of me. "You son of a bitch!" Jacqueline grabbed a glass ashtray off the side table near her and launched it across the room at us. It grazed Keith's head just before it shattered against the wall into tiny pieces. "So this is what you do when I'm not home? You bring hoes into our house to fuck em!"

"Baby I'm sorry! It's not how it looks!"

"Get the hell out of my house and take your tramp with you!"

"Please baby calm down." Keith and I scrambled around the room naked grabbing whatever clothing we could.

"Calm down, I got your calm down." Jacqueline lunged towards me and somehow managed to get a good grip on my hair causing me to wince in pain. "Is this calm enough for you? I'll yank every strand of hair out this hoes head." She was tugging at my hair as if she were in a tug-of-war competition. Doing what I could to fight back, I swung wildly and clawed at the air hoping to connect with some part of her face.

"Let me go!" I yelled feeling my hair being pulled from the roots. Keith grabbed Jacqueline and attempted to pry her hands off my head, but every time he pulled her grip got tighter as she pulled me forward causing me to fall forward. With her hands still locked on my head, I pounded at her face and wherever else I could connect, to get her to let go. Finally connecting to something, I heard her scream and looked to see blood running from her nose.

"That bitch busted my nose." She yelled holding her face.

"Baby, I'm sorry let's talk about this." Keith pled.

"What is there to talk about? You cheat on me with this hoe then think I'm gonna forgive you."

"I ain't gonna be too many more hoes!" I yelled from across the room.

133

"Don't forget you in my house bitch! I could kill your ass if I wanted to and say you were trespassing."

"Baby I swear I'm sorry! Let's sit down and talk about this."

"Keith fuck your sorry! Get your shit and get out of my house!"

"Baby if you just let me explain..." Out of nowhere Jacqueline pulled her hand back and slapped Keith so hard that I could hear it across the room!" He held his face and stared at her blankly not knowing what else to say. Jacqueline looked over at me as if she could read my mind. "Yes honey this is my house. I know you didn't think it was his, now did you? Who do you think decorated it, ain't it obvious?"

"I didn't know he was married!" I yelled.

"Girl please, don't try to act all innocent. You knew he had a woman you just didn't care. It's okay though, I got something for both of y'all."

"Whatever." I waved her off and grabbed my things to leave.

"Y'all aren't moving fast enough!" Jacqueline yelled at us.

"Baby can we at least talk this out?" Keith attempted to grab Jacqueline's hands but she pulled away.

"Keith I'm not playing. Hurry up and get your shit to leave or I'm gonna start throwing it out on the front lawn!" Attempting to make my departure, I walked pass Jacqueline to the front door and she followed behind me. As soon as I opened the door Jacqueline shoved me through it, causing me trip and fall on the front porch.

"Bitch!" I yelled pissed that she got the last laugh. With a frown on my face, I pulled myself up off the concrete and gathered everything that fell from my hands off the ground.

"You wanted him so bad now you got him cuz I'm done with him. I hope you got somewhere for him to live cuz he's gonna need it." A few minutes later, I saw Keith's clothes and things flying out of the second floor window. "Since you wanna cheat get your lying cheating ass out my house!" I watched in disbelief as Jacqueline tossed pants, shoes, and shirts in piles out of the window while yelling obscenities like a mad woman. As I drove off I prayed to God Keith wouldn't call my house trying to ruin my marriage too.

Chapter 15

Tanya

I decided to start looking for a new job, but not before getting some much-needed relaxation for a couple of weeks. Darnelle wasn't thrilled with idea but I figured he'd get over it eventually. Since my hiatus from work, my daily routine has transitioned to getting Danielle up and ready for school in the mornings, seeing Darnelle off to work as a commercial truck driver, and picking Danielle up from school in the evenings. This schedule allows me a lot of free time to myself throughout the day. Considering this, Darnelle tends to go out of his way to keep tabs on me because he feels all the extra time allows me a chance to "explore other options" as he puts it, so this has caused quite a bit of tension between us. Speaking of the devil, here he is calling me again for the umpteenth time. "Hello."

"Hey, what you doing?"

"I'm getting ready to leave for my hair appointment."

"I thought that wasn't until tomorrow."

"My hairstylist changed it to today."

"And when did this happen?"

"A couple of hours ago because she has a doctor's appointment tomorrow evening." I blew out a breath of frustration.

"Yeah okay, if I find out you ain't there you know we're gonna have some problems right?" "Yes father." I mocked him knowing that he hates it when I'm sarcastic.

"I'll call you later." Darnelle abruptly hung up the phone leaving me to listen to the dial tone. Annoyed, I slammed the phone back on the receiver, grabbed my keys and purse then quickly headed out the door.

A few hours later after having my hair straightened and styled, I headed over to the nail salon to get a fill-in and manicure only to receive yet another call from Darnelle.

"Yes Darnelle?"

"Where you at? I came by the hair place, but you weren't there."

"That's because she's finished with my hair, I'm at the nail salon now."

"Which one, I'm coming to meet you."

"Nails Pro, the one up the street from the hair salon."

"Alright I'll be there in ten minutes." Exactly ten minutes later Darnelle walks through the door looking like he just stepped off the set of a rap video.

"Hey baby you get your nails done yet?" Darnelle kissed me on the cheek.

"No the person I usually go to has a client right now so I have to wait till she's done."

"Can't you go to one of these other chicks?" Darnelle

pointed to one of the other nail techs.

"I prefer to stick to the same person."

"Well here goes some money to get your nails and feet done." Darnelle pulled a wad of money out his pocket.

"How much do you need?"

"About sixty dollars." He scanned the room for attention as he counted out three twenties.

"You know what? Don't worry about it baby I got it." I said hoping he'd stop the charade, but still he insisted on giving it to me. Noticing most of the women in the shop staring at him, Darnelle smiled and pulled two more twenties off the money wad to give me. I frowned. "Darnelle who are you showing off for? You never offer to pay for anything."

"I ain't showing off for nobody. I just wanted to do something nice for you."

"Yeah right, what's the real reason behind your special treatment?"

"I just told you, you think I didn't notice you've been stressed out lately?"

"Whatever Darnelle just take your money and go."

"What's your damn problem?" Darnelle grabbed my arm.

"YOU! I'm tired of you putting on fronts for these bitches. If you want somebody else just say the word and you're free."

"See this is why I don't do nothing for you cuz you don't appreciate shit. I guarantee you any of these other women up in here would be happy to take my money and not have to spend theirs." Darnelle eyeballed a few of the women staring at us. It took everything in my power not to smack the hell out him.

"You know what? I'll just come back later cuz I'll be damned if I stand here and get disrespected in front of my face." I turned to leave and Darnelle pulled me back by my arm.

"What the hell are you talking about?"

"You know exactly what I'm talking about. If you want another woman, by all means go get one. Don't think that just because we got Danielle you have to stay here. Believe me we'll be fine with or without you."

"I'm not leaving my daughter."

"You can come see her as much as you want but I will not continue to put up with this shit!"

"What shit Tanya?" Darnelle stared at me as if I were crazy.

"You trying to pick up hoes while I'm with you! You think I didn't see how those women were staring at you. That's why you pulled that money out. To show them you got it like that."

Darnelle waved me off. "Man please you can gone with all that. It's not my fault they were looking at me."

"It's sad you think I'm stupid enough to believe that you didn't pull that money out to impress those women. I'm not a fool. It's not like this is the first time we've had issues with you dealing with other women."

"You talking crazy now." Darnelle smirked.

"Oh I clearly remember finding a few phone numbers in your pants pockets when I was washing our clothes a few months back."

"That's because you were snooping through my stuff. That's what happens when you look for shit. You find stuff you don't wanna find."

"I was clearing out your pockets to wash your clothes when I found those numbers so don't try to make it seem like I was going through your stuff. Wash your own clothes next time and you won't get caught up!"

He grabbed me by my neck. "You ain't finna be up in here talking to me crazy trying to embarrass me."

"Fuck you Darnelle!" I spat while gasping for oxygen.

"Hey, hey you need to leave," one of the nail techs said with a strong Asian accent. "I call the police!" Everyone else looked on in shock as if it was a live soap opera playing right before their eyes. "You need leave now! Police on their way!" The lady reiterated.

"I heard you!" Darnelle yelled then practically dragged me out of the door by my arm. "We gonna finish this at home. Get in the car." He barked at me.

"I ain't going nowhere with you."

Darnelle looked around and notice people starting to stare. "Get in the damn car."

"No!" I yelled to the top of my lungs. "Get away from me!" I yanked away from him then walked off briskly leaving him standing there looking stupid. Embarrassed, he hopped in the car and sped off.

After having my day ruined by Darnelle, I hopped in my car and decided to go home and try to relax. I ran me a nice warm bath, turned on some music, and prepared for my much-needed aromatherapy. After a half hour of relaxing in the tub, I washed up and began drying off.

"Tanya!" I heard Darnelle yell from downstairs as he slammed the door behind him. I sighed as I put my robe on. *Here we go again.* Darnelle burst through the bathroom door.

"Where you been?"

"What you mean where I been? I've been here." Irritated, I brushed pass him. He followed me down the hall and into the bedroom.

"You didn't come straight here cuz I came by here after you stormed off. So where did you go?"

"I already told you I came here. If you don't believe me that's your problem. Now I'm going to bed." I tried to leave the bedroom, but he grabbed my arm. "Let me go Darnelle!"

"When we finish talking I will, but you're gonna tell me where you went first."

"I already told you. Now let me go!" I tried to jerk away, but he pulled me back.

"You kill me Darnelle. You can go out collect numbers and do whatever else you wanna do and I'm not supposed to question you. But it's okay for you to keep questioning me?" We stood face to face staring each other down.

"That's cuz you lying."

"What I got to lie about Darnelle? For real just get out my face." I pulled away and pushed him out of my way. Before I could take a step he grabbed me by the back of my neck.

"I'm sick of playing these games with you. You embarrass me in front of all those people then lie about coming home afterward. You better tell me something." He tightened his grip on my neck causing me to scream out in pain.

"Darnelle you're hurting me! Please let go." He escorted me down the hall and into the bedroom with the grip of a boa constrictor on the back of my neck.

"You better start talking," he said through gritted teeth.

"I don't have shit to tell you! What you want me to make something up!" Tears started to form in my eyes from the grip he had on my neck.

"You got one more time to lie to me! I ain't gonna ask you again." Worried I pondered what to do next when I noticed a demonic look in his eyes.

"I don't know what else to say Danielle. I told you the truth, but you don't believe me!" He grabbed me by my throat and slammed me on the bed. "You lying bitch!" I lay on the bed clawing at him and gasping for air as he squeezed my neck even tighter. I dug my nails into his skin until I was able to draw blood then I raked my nails across his right eye. "Aahh you fucking bitch!" He yelled out in pain holding his eye. I took advantage of the opportunity and leaped off the bed. I ran out of the room and down the hall, but Darnelle was on my trail. I tried running to the kitchen to grab a knife, but as soon as my foot hit the bottom step Darnelle yanked me back by my hair.

"Aahh", I yelled out in pain. He dragged me up the steps as I kicked and screamed and attempted to pry his hands out of my hair. When he finally got to the top of the stairs he dropped me to the floor and stood over me.

"You thought you was gonna get away with lying to me in my face!" He drew his fist back and punched me so hard in my face that my jaw went numb. I was so dazed that when I tried to scream out in pain no sound came of my mouth. Darnelle continued to stand over me yelling about how I lied to him. "Answer me!" He yelled, but I had no clue what he asked me. "Oh you not gonna answer me!" He punched me again then kicked me in my stomach. I turned on my side and clenched up into a ball on the floor to ease the pain and cushion the blows.

"Please stop!" I cried then put my hands up in surrender but he hit me again.

"Where were you?"

"I went to check on Danielle at school before I came to the house." I lied knowing it was the only way to get him to stop. He grabbed me by my chin and forced me to face him. "Look me in my face and tell me that shit." I repeated what I said while he stared at me as if he was attempting to read my thoughts. Not knowing what else to say or do, he let my face go and headed back towards the bedroom.

Bleeding and in pain, I stumbled to my feet and wobbled towards the bathroom. I locked the door behind me and looked at myself in the mirror. I dabbed my swollen, bloody face with a wet towel then sat on the toilet and softly cried to myself. *What have I gotten myself into?* I held my face in my hands and refused to leave the bathroom.

About ten minutes later I heard the front door slam so I rushed over to the bathroom window. I pulled the blinds back and watched Darnelle pull out of the driveway. Once he got down the street, I quickly darted out of the bathroom and threw on a sweat suit. I grabbed my suitcase and began filling it with as many of Danielle and my clothes as I could and then rushed to my car. *I gotta get out of here or next time I might not be so lucky.*

I frantically dialed my sister, Niki, on her cell phone as I pulled out of the driveway. *Please pick up the phone.* "Hey sis?" Niki answered causing me to feel a sense of relief.

"Hey are you at home right now?"

"No, but I'll be there in about half an hour."

"Would you mind if Danielle and I come over for a while?"

"Of course not. You can come over whenever you want."

"Okay I'm gonna swing by Danielle's school to pick her up then we'll meet at your place."

"Actually I'll be going past there on my way home. I can pick her up for you if you want me to."

"That'll be great, thank you." A couple tears escaped from my eyes as I silently thanked Niki for picking Danielle up for me. The last thing I wanted was for my baby to see me all banged up like this then having to figure out a way to explain to her what happened.

I sat in Niki's driveway for fifteen minutes before she pulled up but to prevent Danielle from seeing me all battered and bruised up I remained in the car. A couple of minutes later Niki tapped on my driver-side window. I rolled it down just enough for her to see my sunshades. "Hey, are you coming in?"

"Yeah just give me a minute."

"Alright I'm a go ahead and take Danielle in the house, I'll see you in a minute."

I watched as Niki escorted Danielle to the front door and into the house. About ten minutes later I got out of the car and crept inside the house. As I tiptoed into the kitchen, I felt a tap on my shoulder, which startled me.

"What you doing?" Niki asked me curiously.

"Nothing, about to grab something to drink. Where's Danielle?"

"She's in the room watching cartoons. What's going on

with you? Ever since you got here you've been acting strange."

"Things aren't going so well." I gave a halfhearted smile. Niki poured herself a glass of juice and sat down at the dining room table.

"Come sit down so we can talk." Niki patted the seat across from her. I slowly walked over to the dining room and sat down.

"Now what's going on? And please take off those shades." Niki laughed lightly. I hesitantly took my sunglasses off and Niki gasped. "Oh my God, who did this to you? What happened?" She walked over and began examining my cuts and bruises as I choked back tears.

"Darnelle, we got into it and one thing led to another then next thing you know we were fighting."

"No, it's more like you became his punching bag." Niki frowned up her face in anger. "So Darnelle did this to you?" Niki held my chin as she examined my bruises "I knew something wasn't right about that bastard. Is this the first time he's hit you?"

"No." I mumbled.

"Why didn't you tell me before, did you call the police?"

"No, I came straight over here."

Niki gave me a look of disappointment. "I'm gonna see if Mrs. Miller next door can watch Danielle for a minute cuz you need to go to the hospital to get those cuts looked at. Was that asshole...I mean was Darnelle there when you left?"

"No, I waited till he left because I knew if he was still there he wouldn't let me leave."

"You should've called the cops on his ass." Niki frowned and grabbed her jacket. "I'll be right back." Niki headed next door to talk to Mrs. Miller. Five minutes later she returned with Mrs. Miller and gestured for me to come over.

"You're right; she needs to go get that looked at." Mrs. Miller said sympathetically while looking at my face. "I'd ask you how you've been but from the looks of it, not well. I can't believe Darnelle did this to you. He seemed like such a nice man." Mrs. Miller has been a good friend of the family for quite some time, so I wasn't surprised when Niki told her about what happened between Darnelle and me. She pretty much knows everything that happens in the family and is always there to lend an ear or helping hand. "Anyway y'all go ahead to the hospital. Danielle can stay here with me for the night to give you time to handle things. Call and let me know what happens."

"Thanks Mrs. Miller, will do." I smiled.

When we arrived at the hospital, they had me fill out some forms and sit in the waiting room. "I need to check on Danielle. What if he tries to come get her?"

"Don't worry I already told Mrs. Miller that under no circumstances is he allowed to take her. And that she should call the cops if he gets stupid. In my neighborhood the cops don't play. If you call them, they're there in like five minutes, if that long. So you have absolutely nothing to worry about." Niki reassured me.

We waited for a half hour before I was finally called back to see the doctor. A nurse took my vitals and escorted me to a room then shortly after a tall, slim Caucasian man who introduced himself as Dr. Gables came in and examined me. He informed me that I would need stitches to close up the wounds on my head and underneath my left eye.

"So how did this happen?" He asked me curiously.

"Me and my husband had a dispute."

"So he did this to you?" Dr. Gables quizzed.

"Unfortunately yes." I sniffed back tears.

After stitching my wounds, Dr. Gables looked at me sympathetically. "I'll be back in one minute." He said then left the room. He returned a few minutes later with two police officers. I stared at Dr. Gables in disbelief.

"Why are they here?"

"I thought they might be able to help you." He said unable to look me in the eyes.

"Mrs. Fuller, I'm Officer Ross and this is Officer Ford. Dr. Gables was concerned and thought you might want to file a report."

I let out a nervous breath of air and shook my head. "I don't know if I want to do that."

"What do you mean? He beat the hell out of you. Have you seen your face?" Niki said to me frustrated while looking at me as if I were crazy.

"I'm just scared. What's gonna happen if I go through with this?"

"There's nothing to be scared of Mrs. Fuller. We're just gonna ask you a few questions for the report." I hesitantly agreed and wondered if I was doing the right thing.

"So when and where did the confrontation between you and your husband take place?"

"Around 5:30 p.m. at our house." I wrote down our address.

"What happened exactly?"

I ran down the story of how the fight began and ended as

tears streamed down my cheeks. "I've had issues with him putting his hands on me before, but never to this extent." I cried as Niki handed me some tissue and patted my back. "I'm sorry y'all. I just get so upset talking about it." I dabbed my eyes with tissue.

"It's ok Mrs. Fuller. We know this is hard for you to explain. You've given us enough for the report," Officer Doss replied. "Would you be able to give us your husband's name?"

"What's gonna happen if I give you his name?"

"We'll put a warrant out for his arrest and he'll probably serve a few days in jail until you decide whether or not you want to press charges." I sighed as I considered what to do. "Okay, his name is Darnelle Fuller." Officer Ford wrote down the information I gave him and detached a copy of his report.

"Here's your copy of the police report and my card. The address to the police department is attached." I took the report and card from Officer Ford, put them in my purse, and stood up to leave.

"Excuse me Mrs. Fuller."

"Yes." I turned around to face Officer Ford's partner, Officer Doss.

"If you have any questions or problems please give me a call, here's my card as well."

"Thank you." I gave Officer Doss a slight smile then reached to take the card from him but he didn't let it go. He held on to the other end for a minute and gazed at me for a moment before finally letting it go.

"Thank you." I looked at him oddly then grabbed my things to leave. After Officer Doss and Ford left I breathed a sigh of relief. I was happy that they were finally gone.

"Mrs. Fuller I apologize for catching you off guard by bringing the officers in, but I thought they might be able to help you. I try not to stick my nose in my patient's business, but every now and then I have to do what I feel is right, hopefully you understand."

"No it's fine Dr. Gables, thank you." We shared an awkward silence.

"Well here's your appointment card be sure to come back so I can take those stitches out."

"Will do Doc. Thank you again." Though it was not his job to stick his nose in my business, I did appreciate him being concerned. Besides, I never would've filed the report had he not brought the officers in even though it was something that needed to be done to show Darnelle I would not continue to take his abuse.

After leaving the hospital, Niki insisted that I stay with her till I figured out my next move. Happy I agreed to stay, Niki fixed the spare bedroom for me and I quickly dozed off to sleep. The next morning around nine o'clock, she practically dragged me out of the bed and rushed me to get dressed. "Girl what is your problem and where are you taking me that's so important?"

"Don't worry about it. You'll find out when we get there, just hurry up and get dressed." After getting dressed, Niki rushed me out to the car and peeled out of the driveway.

"Girl are you crazy, what is wrong with you? And you know I gotta get Danielle from Mrs. Miller."

"I already took care of that. Mrs. Miller said she's good and we can come get her when we're ready."

"Okay, but where are you taking me?" I looked at Niki

quizzically knowing she was up to something.

"I'm taking you to do something you should've done a long time ago."

I blew out a breath of air. "Oh Lord! What are you up to?"

Twenty minutes later we pull up in the parking lot of a gun shop, I looked at Niki. "Are you getting another gun?" I crossed my arms across my chest.

"No, we're getting you a gun for protection."

"Niki that's crazy. Now you know how I feel about having guns around Danielle." I looked at her as if she lost her mind.

"Put the gun in a safe place where she can't reach it and lock it up. Or better yet, keep it on you. That way you'll know where it is at all times."

"Niki that's illegal."

"Not if it's registered. Just keep it unloaded and locked up in a case in your trunk."

"What'll be the point of carrying it if I gotta do all that?"

"It's the comfort of knowing you can protect yourself if you need to."

"Niki I swear you got some kind of gun fetish. You already then shot one person." I laughed lightly.

"You can laugh if you want but Shawn deserved it. Just think what could've happened if I didn't have that gun… I mean seriously Tanya look at what Darnelle did to you, next time you might not be so lucky. You could end up in the hospital in a coma or even worse, dead. If you have a gun the next time he decides to use you for a punching bag you can protect yourself. Believe me that fool may not back off when you threaten him, but when you do it with that gun he will or at least think twice about what he's gonna do."

"Niki, I'm not trying to go to jail for killing nobody."

"I'm not telling you to kill him. If you end up having to shoot him just aim for his arm or leg that way he'll know you mean business. That'll definitely cause him to think twice about hitting you…"

"I don't know Niki I've never even held a gun before and I definitely don't know how to shoot one."

"Don't worry we'll work on all that. Just trust me." After giving it some thought, I decided to at least go in the store and talk to someone before completely ruling out the idea.

"Hey Niki! How you doing today? We haven't seen you in a while." I looked on as Niki shook the store manager's hand.

"Yeah I know. I've been backed up with cases for work lately so I haven't had a lot of free time."

"Well we're happy to see you. Now what can I help you with today?"

"Actually, I'm here for my sister today. She's looking for something small like a .22 or a .25."

"Sounds good, let me show you what we have." The store manager escorted us over to a glass case that was filled with various handguns.

"I found it. This would be perfect for you." Niki pointed to a small silver pistol.

"What kind of gun is that?" I stared at the pocket size pistol.

"It's a .25 semi-automatic pistol." The store manager explained to me as he unlocked the case and took it out. "See that would be great. It's just big enough for you to handle." I held it and stared at it for a minute.

"How much is it?"

"Four hundred and fifty dollars..." The store manager said.

"So what you think?" The store manager smiled slightly.

"It's perfect we'll take it." Niki answered grinning from ear to ear.

"Hold up Niki. I don't know."

"Tanya I will teach you everything you need to know from how to hold it to how to shoot it. I'm telling you it will be fine..."

I sighed. "Okay, I'll take it."

"Now it's gonna take about a week for us to verify your information so we'll give you a call to come pick it up." The store manager smiled. "You paying with cash or credit?"

"Credit I guess." I hadn't planned on spending that type of money today so I shuffled around in my purse trying to figure out whether I should get it now or wait, especially considering the circumstances of my job. After watching me shuffling around in my purse for a couple of minutes Niki walked over. She kindly pulled my purse out of my hand and closed it up. "Don't worry about it I got it."

"Niki that's a lot of money."

"It's not a problem Tanya, besides I'm the one that talked you into getting it." Niki handed the store manager her card.

"Thank you Niki."

"Don't mention it." She smiled.

Before we left, the store manager explained that I would have to take a gun safety course online and gave me the information for the website. "Now you're gonna have to take this before I'm able to give you your handgun, so try to get it done as soon as possible."

"Okay, thank you." I smiled and wondered what I'd just gotten myself into.

Chapter 16

Candy

I lay in bed thinking about Taye and the great time we had on our date. It's been about a week since I've seen or heard from him so I decide to call him to see what's up. But before I can dial his number completely I hear someone tap on my bedroom door. As I was getting up to throw on my robe Tia cracks the door and pokes her head in. "Hey I know it's early, but I have something important to talk to you about, can you come downstairs for a minute?"

"Sure what's up? We can talk in here if you want."

Tia gave me an uneasy look and said, "No that's okay. I'd rather you come downstairs."

"Um okay, give me a few minutes to throw something on." After I put on some sweats and a t-shirt I stopped in the room next to mine to check on SJ. After seeing that he was sleeping peacefully, I continued downstairs and took a seat across from Tia in the living room.

"So what's up?" I stared at her and attempted to read her

expression.

"I just wanted to tell you that I know things have been hard for you living in a new city and not having a steady man in your life, but Thomas is not up for grabs…"

"Excuse me!" I looked at her like she was crazy and she put her hand up to stop me from talking.

"Wait a minute let me finish. I let you stay here because I knew you needed somewhere to live until you get settled in and I trusted that you wouldn't cause an issue in my relationship so with that said…"

"What do you mean Thomas isn't up for grabs? I don't want him. If I wanted a man I'd have one, I don't need to take yours." At this point, I knew this heffa had lost her mind.

"Well Thomas told me how you came on to him the other day in the hallway and you being my cousin, I expected more from you."

"So instead of you asking me if it's true you automatically believe him?"

"What reason would he have to lie?" I clinched my fist wanting to knock some sense into her. "Thomas is lying to you. I never came on to him. While he was telling you all that, did he bother telling you how I caught him messing around with a stripper in your car…." We both looked up and saw Thomas coming downstairs. "Since he's up, maybe you should ask him." I smirked.

"What's going on? I heard y'all down here yelling."

"You're right on time. Why don't you tell Tia about that stripper I caught you with that night I saw you at the strip club." I glared at him.

"What stripper?" Thomas pretended to look confused.

"Thomas don't play stupid you know exactly what I'm talking about. And when exactly did I come on to you cuz this is news to me."

"Thomas is this true?" Tia looked at him with pleading eyes.

"No, it's not true. She's just saying that to take the heat off her."

"That's bullshit Thomas and you know it! I caught you in the parking lot in Tasha's car, with a stripper or should I say with Bubbles' at the club getting a blowjob.

"If this is true why didn't you tell me the night you caught him?" Tia asked me.

"He said he was gonna tell you. I told him he had two days to come clean or I'd tell you myself."

"Okay it's a week later now." Tia looked at me.

"I had every intention to tell you, but I've been so busy working. I haven't had a chance to."

"Honestly I don't know which one of you is telling the truth, but for now I think it would be best if you found somewhere else to stay."

"For real though you're gonna take his word over mine? I can't believe this shit! I'm blood he's not. How you gonna kick me out for his lying ass?"

"I'm just done with all y'all drama so to end it all I'd rather you leave."

"Why not him? Are you that desperate to have a man?"

"I just think this is best, now I'm done discussing it." Tia walked out and I followed behind her. "If that's how you want it that's fine, but don't come calling and crying to me when you find out how much of a lying cheating bastard he is. I'd also advise you to go get tested because it's a good chance he's got something. Hopefully, for your sake it's curable. I stormed upstairs, grabbed my suitcases, and immediately started packing. A few minutes later, I heard a tap on my door. Tia stuck her head in and then stood in the doorway with a guilty look on her face. "Can I talk to you for a minute?"

"There's nothing else to talk about. You've said what you had to say so I'm done with it." I continued to pack my suitcase.

"I'm sorry Candy it's just that..."

"It's just that what Tia? It's clear who's more important to you so just gone back downstairs with your man and leave me alone because I'm done talking."

"I just want to know if what you said is true Candy, please don't shut me out." I looked at her and laughed lightly. "Why don't you ask him? I'm sure he'll tell you everything you want to know. Now if you don't mind I need to finish packing." Tia continued to stand in the doorway but after a few minutes of me ignoring her she finally left. It hurts like hell to know my cousin cares more about her dude than me but karma is a bitch and soon enough she'll see that she made the wrong decision and its gonna tear her up inside, if it isn't already.

I didn't have anywhere to go so I phoned Taye in hopes that he could help me out but when I called him, he didn't answer. Weighing what little options I had, I began calling around for hotel prices and eventually settled on a Motel 6 that was in the area. After loading all my things in the car, which wasn't much, I went back upstairs to grab SJ who was still quietly sleeping. I didn't want to wake him so I slowly picked him up and carefully walked him downstairs. As I tried to walk past Tia she reached out her hands to grab him. "I'm good I don't need your help." I turned my nose up at her and continued walking to my car.

"Let her go, she got it." Thomas said to Tia with a slight smirk on his face. Even though I was angry as hell, I calmly strapped SJ into his car seat, cracked the windows so he could get some air, and then headed back inside the house.

When I walked through the front door Tia asked, "Did you forget something?"

"Yes Tia, I did." I calmly walked over to Thomas and slapped him so hard that I could see my hand print on the side of his pale face. "When my cousin finds out the truth I hope she kicks your ass from sun up to sun down and sends you packing with nowhere to go just like she did me." I glared at him daring him to hit me back. "Have a nice life." I walked past Tia with tear-filled eyes and shook my head as I headed out the door.

Thankful that the Motel 6 I chose wasn't too shabby, I laid SJ down on the bed and sat next to him. "I guess it's just me and you now sweetheart." I looked at him, smiled slightly and caressed his cheek. After a few minutes my phone rang. It was Taye.

"Hey what you doing?"

"Nothing, I'm over here a Motel 6 unpacking some of my things."

"What you doing there? Don't tell me you there with some dude."

"No Taye I'm not. What would it matter to you anyway? You haven't called me since we went out."

"I've been busy recording music in the studio."

"Well you could've at least called me." I snapped.

"I ain't got time to be arguing with you, I'll just talk to you later."

"Taye wait, I'm sorry please don't hang up." I began to tear up.

"Candy what's wrong, why you crying?"

I sniffed back tears and paused for a minute to get myself together.

"Candy?" Taye called thinking I hung up.

"I'm here."

"What happened?"

"Tia... kicked me out for her husband Thomas."

"The fool you had issues with the other night?"

"Yes." I wiped away more tears. "Now I'm stuck staying here at Motel 6 because it's the only place I can afford."

"Candy which one are you at?"

"The one near Lucky's Gas Station on..."

"Don't worry I know where you are. I'll be there in about fifteen minutes." Twenty minutes later Taye knocked on the door.

"Hey, how did you know which room I was in I never even told you my room number?"

"I just asked the dude at the front desk."

"What if you were some type of psycho killer or something I'd be dead right now."

"My point exactly, it's not safe here." Taye looked at me concerned. "I don't have a choice but to stay here, I have nowhere else to go." I plopped down on the bed.

"So what happened?" Taye sat down in a chair next to my bed.

"He lied and told her I tried to come on to him the other

day."

"And she believed him?" Taye looked at me confused.

"Apparently yes or I'd still be there."

"Did you tell her about the stripper you caught him with?"

"Of course I did but as she said, she couldn't tell which one of us was telling the truth so she thought it would be best if I just left. I guess she felt it was easier screwing me over than facing up to the problem and being without a man."

"Do you have any family here other than Tia?"

"Yeah, but none that'll actually let me stay with them. We've never been close so I barely even talk to them."

"So what are you gonna do?"

I looked at Taye annoyed and hurt then sighed. "I'm gonna stay here until I find a place to live." Taye got out of his chair and began pacing the floor, then looked at me with a sincere expression on his face. "Taye you alright?" He didn't answer for a minute then finally he sighed and picked up one of my suitcases off the floor.

"Grab your things."

"Why, I just finished unpacking everything."

"Because it's not safe for you to stay here especially with a three year old."

"Where the hell else am I gonna go Taye? I'm kinda limited on options you know." I stood up facing him and folded my arms across my chest.

"Just stop asking questions and grab your things, you're coming with me." I couldn't help the smile that spread across my face from the surprising news. "Taye are you sure about this?"

"Candy just grab your things before I change my mind."

"Yes sir." I smiled again as I began repacking my things and couldn't help but be turned on by the way he took charge of the situation. I love a man who takes charge it makes me feel secure. *I guess he has a heart after all.* I laughed to myself.

After riding for about thirty minutes, we pulled up in front of a cute secluded townhouse complex out in the suburbs. I walked quietly behind Taye with SJ in my arms as he escorted me inside the house and to his guest bedroom, which had a queen sized bed and a 42 inch flat screen TV hanging from the wall. I walked around the room admiring the baby blue and white walls that were neatly decorated with various pictures of jazz musicians and people dancing.

"Here are a few toys for SJ to play with just in case he gets bored." Taye handed SJ a stuffed teddy bear.

"You're quite the family man from what I see, I never would of thought it." I smiled at him.

"Me and my wife were planning on having a kid before she passed away, as you can see she got a little ahead of herself." Taye laughed lightly as he reminisced. "She figured that at least the room would be ready whenever it happened. There used to be crib in here too, but I replaced it with the bed and turned this into a guest room."

"Well it's a really nice room and I appreciate you letting us stay here. I promise we'll do our best to stay out of your way, you won't even notice we're here."

"It's all good I don't mind helping, besides I wouldn't have felt right letting you stay there." Taye smiled.

"Well thank you again." Taye and I stared at each other for a minute then smiled.

"I'm gonna let you go ahead and get unpacked just come downstairs when you're ready and I'll have dinner for you."

After about an hour I came downstairs with SJ. "Hey you hungry? I ordered some pizza and wings. I thought maybe we could watch a movie or something."

"Sure that sounds great."

After choosing a movie to watch, Taye sat on the couch next to me and SJ then got comfortable. After we watched at least three movies, I noticed SJ starting to doze off. "I'm gonna lay him down real quick, I'll be right back." A few minutes later, I returned and sat next to Taye. We watched one more movie then began talking about our family, friends, and past relationships. Our conversation didn't end till almost two in the morning. I watched as Taye got up off the couch and stretched.

"I'm gonna head to bed so you can get some rest. I know you're probably tired, especially after everything you went through today."

"Yeah a little." I yawned. Taye walked me upstairs to my room.

"Have a good night's sleep. I'll see you in the morning."

"Okay...Taye?" He turned around when I called his name. "Thank you for everything. I don't know how I could ever repay you." I smiled sincerely.

"By getting back on your feet and making a better life for you and SJ." He smiled. "Good night Candy." Taye walked out of the room and quietly closed the door behind him. After that, I prayed and thanked God for sending such a wonderful man to help me out in my time of need. Then I lay down like Taye suggested so I could get some rest.

I woke up the next morning to the smell of pancakes, eggs, and bacon, which instantly caused my stomach to growl. I breathed in the scent of fresh breakfast. *Umm that smells good.* Unable to ignore the tantalizing smell any longer, I instantly scooped SJ up in my arms and let my nose lead the way to the kitchen. I admired Taye's home once again as I walked down the stairs. I loved his townhouse, it wasn't too big but not too small either and it felt so comfortable. I couldn't help but feel at home here. "Good morning." I smiled at Taye as I peeked my head into the kitchen.

"Hey, come in and have a seat. I made us some breakfast. How'd you sleep last night?"

"Great, it was the best sleep I've had in a while." I sat SJ in his high chair in the dining room and sat in a chair next to him. Taye's kitchen opened up to the dining room making it easy to talk and see everything while you're cooking. "You gotta work today?" Taye asked as he sat a plate of food down in front of me.

"I'm supposed to go in at one o'clock, but that's only if the new stripper they just hired doesn't show up. If I don't have to go in today I'm gonna go apartment hunting."

"Candy you don't have to rush, I'm fine with y'all being here. Take your time and get situated."

"But I don't want to impose…"

"You're not. I live by myself so you're cool." Taye sat on the opposite side of SJ and began cutting his pancakes into squares. After eating breakfast, I took a shower and got ready for work. Taye met me at the bottom of the stairs.

"So what are you gonna do with SJ while you're at work?"

"There's a lady I take him to that runs a daycare. She's not cheap, but at least I know he's in safe hands."

"If you don't mind I can ask my Aunt Gloria to watch him while you're gone."

"I don't know Taye. I don't want to burden her."

"I promise it won't be a bother. She loves kids and plus it'll save you money."

I contemplated his suggestion for a minute. "Well... I guess."

Taye called her while I waited in the living room for her response. He came back with a smile on his face. "She said she'd love to watch him and she'd be over to pick him up in twenty minutes." Fifteen minutes later Gloria picked SJ up and I was headed out the door, but before I could get my foot on the front porch my phone rang.

"What wrong?" Taye asked me noticing the disappointed look on my face as I took the call.

"Nothing. That was my job. I don't have to work today."

"So why do you look mad then?"

"Because I need money." I plopped down on the living room sofa.

"See, if you get a regular job you won't have that problem because your paycheck comes regularly."

"Yeah you got a point there." I looked at Taye and sighed.

"I guess I'm gonna go ahead and check out a few apartments."

"Why don't you come with me, we can check out a few spots while we're out."

"Where are we going?"

"Out." Taye smiled. "Now grab your purse." He said then dragged me towards the door by my hand.

Chapter 17

Mason

The first thing I saw after I finally snapped back to reality after being in a coma for a week was Charlene sleeping in a chair next to my bed holding my hand. Not wanting to wake her, I quietly lay in bed and watched her sleep. But as if she could sense I was awake, she slowly parted her eyes.

"Mason?" Charlene squinted from the light as she looked at me. "Oh my God! I'm so glad you're awake! I gotta call Niki and Donte." Charlene hugged me tightly.

"I didn't miss my babies being born did I?"

"Of course you didn't' baby." I looked down noticing Charlene's belly had gotten a little bigger, I smiled and began to rub it.

"So what happened?"

"You don't remember?" Charlene looked at me a bit surprised. "You got shot at the gym where you and Donte were playing basketball. Donte said it was some dude named Trevon that did it."

"Did they get him?"

"The police caught him a few blocks away from the gym."

"How long have you been here?"

"Ever since you got in the hospital. Other than going home every now and then to grab a few things I've been here the whole time." She caressed my face and stared at me as a single tear rolled down her cheek. "I missed you so much Mason. All I could think about was our kids growing up without a father."

I grabbed Charlene's hand and kissed it. "I'll never leave you baby, I want to see our kids grow up just as much as you do." We talked a little more and then Charlene called Donte and Niki.

They walked in thirty minutes later with balloons, a gift basket, and a card that read *Get Well Soon.* "Hey stranger." Niki smiled as she walked over and gave me a hug and kiss on the cheek. "How you feeling?"

"In pain, I never imagined I'd be in the hospital for getting shot. I can be a rapper now since that seems to be the trend." I laughed.

"Nice to know you still got your sense of humor." Donte smiled and gave me a brotherly hug. "I'm sorry about what happened I wish there was more I could've done..." I put my hand up to stop Donte from talking.

"Man there was only so much you could do it's not your fault this happened. None of us knew he was coming back like that. He'll get his though, even if I can't get at him... Now what y'all bring me to eat? I'm hungry as hell and this hospital food ain't where it's at." Everyone laughed as I rubbed my stomach.

"How you just gonna change the subject like that?" Donte laughed.

Two weeks later, I was out of the hospital and attending physical therapy three times a week. "I bet you in two more weeks I'll be walking again." I told Charlene as we rode from my doctor's appointment.

"Keep thinking like that and I'm sure you will baby." Charlene smiled at me as she pulled into our driveway. A few minutes later I received a phone call. After hanging up I looked over to find Charlene staring at me.

"You alright baby?"

"Yeah, that was Donte. He said the dude that shot me got killed."

"So why the look of confusion?"

"I don't know what to think. I just don't want the cops to come looking for me thinking I did it or had something to do with it."

"Why would they think you did it? You were on bed rest this whole time."

"Yeah but they might think I put somebody up to it." A cop car pulled into the driveway behind us as Charlene helped me out of the car and into my wheelchair.

"Good evening. Are you Mason Clark?" One of the two cops asked as they walked towards us with their hands on their guns.

"Yes, that's me."

"May we come in and speak to you for a minute?"

"Sure just give us a minute." Charlene grabbed the rest of my bags out of the car and sat them in my lap. "Follow me officers." I felt my palms getting sweaty as a nervous feeling developed in the pit of my stomach. Once inside, Charlene gestured for the two cops to have a seat on the sofa and then after positioning my wheelchair she sat down next to me in a chair. "So what can I help you with officers?"

"As you might or might not know Trevon Taylor, the man who shot you, was killed this morning. We found his body in a dumpster after receiving a call from the Department of Waste Management. Supposedly, a couple of sanitation workers discovered his body while emptying out a dumpster on one of their routine routes. Now you don't have to pretend to be sympathetic, but we need to know the last time you saw him."

"The day he shot me. I was taken straight to the hospital and I was in a coma for like a week. I haven't seen or heard from him since." The officers then called out a list of names that they had written on a notepad and asked if any of them sounded familiar to me. "No officer they don't, none of those names ring a bell."

"The reason we're asking these questions is because all of these men were taken in for a drug bust early this morning and we think Trevon used to run with them. When we found him, he had been shot three times in the chest and once in the head. It just so happens that one of our witnesses saw him in a car with the guys I named right before the drug bust went down and immediately after he turned up dead in a dumpster. Seeing how you got shot two weeks prior to his death we have to make sure you weren't tied into it."

"I can assure you I had nothing to do with it and if you need to search my home or phone records to prove it then do what you have to do. I ain't never sold or messed around with no drugs so I have nothing to hide." Surprised by my willingness to cooperate, the officers agreed to make their search of my house quick. After calling for backup, they went from room to room looking for anything they could find. After turning up empty handed in the house, they searched my car. Finally completing their search, the officers approached me and said they'd get back with me after reviewing my phone records. A couple of days later they had me come down to the police station to tell me that they found absolutely nothing and my phone records were clean so I was off the hook. Thankful to be off the hook and not have to worry about Trevon any longer, I slept well that night.

The next morning around ten o'clock I met up with Donte to try on tuxes for the wedding. "So what color are we looking for?" I asked Donte as I picked up a tux and put it in front of me.

"Niki wants to go with royal blue so I figured we'd have a white tux and royal blue vests and neck ties."

"That sounds cool." I put the tux I had back on the rack. "Donte can I ask you something."

"Yeah what's up?"

"How did you know Trevon got killed?"

"I saw it on the news."

"But it wasn't on the news." Donte didn't respond he just continued looking at tuxes. "Did you know the dudes that did it?"

"A couple of them. Let's just say they owed me a favor and once he made bail he was fair game."

"So you set him up?"

"I wasn't gonna let him get away with that shit Mason. Plus I knew you couldn't do nothing so I did. You're like a brother to me so I couldn't let that shit ride."

"So what about the other dudes that got locked up and the

169

drug bust?" I whispered trying not to draw attention to us.

"I had nothing to do with the drug bust. I didn't even know about it and as far as the other dudes that got arrested they got money to get a lawyer so they'll be alright." Donte continued tux shopping as if the discussion never took place. I looked at him with a newfound respect and appreciation. I always looked at him like my brother and we've always been close. But after this, I considered him more than just my friend I considered him my blood. I could never repay him for what he did, and because of this he will always be family to me through thick and thin.

Two weeks later, everything was back to normal. My divorce from Ariel was finalized and I'm close to walking again without needing assistance. I was relaxing on my sofa waiting until it was time for my physical therapy appointment. The moment I switched on the TV and got comfortable my phone rang. The caller ID showed an unfamiliar number. I was reluctant to answer it so I stared at the phone for a minute then decided I'd go ahead and see who it was. "Hello."

"So how does it feel being divorced and all?"

"Why are you calling me Ariel? You no longer have that privilege."

"I just wanted to let you know that Nate misses you and so do I. I really messed up when I lost you." Ariel sniffed as if she was crying but I knew that was all a ploy to get me to feel sorry for her. "You were a great man and an even better husband and I'm sorry I didn't realize that when we were together. I know you're not interested in hearing all this but I had to get this off my chest."

"Okay so are you done now?" I rubbed my face irritated.

"No, I want to know if you would mind paying Nate a

visit. He always asks about you. I understand that what we have is over, but you're the closest thing to a father he's ever had."

"I'm sorry I can't do that. I don't want him thinking I'm gonna be around when I'm not. He's probably already having issues with me being gone and I don't want to confuse him anymore than he already is."

"He needs a good man in his life Mason."

"Okay, so where is his real father? Didn't you find him?"

"Yes, but he already has a family of his own that he needs to get situated with the news so he can't be here for Nate the way he should until he tells them about him."

"The man was married?"

"Yes, him and his new wife recently had a baby so he hasn't told her about Nate yet."

I smirked in disbelief and shook my head. "Well I'm getting ready to have a family too so I can't help you."

"What do you mean you getting ready to have a family too?" Ariel mimicked me.

"Charlene is pregnant with twins, *my* twins. So I have my own life to live and worry about."

"She's pregnant?" I could hear the anger in Ariel's voice radiate through the phone. "You neglected to say that at the divorce hearing. So when exactly did this happen?"

"I don't have to explain nothing to you. We're not together anymore."

"You're full of shit Mason! You don't have to make up lies to keep from seeing Nate."

"Why would I need to lie to you? Besides you put yourself in this position when you cheated on me so this is your problem to solve not mine."

"So you really got her pregnant?"

"Man get off my phone I don't have time for this shit. Good luck with dude cuz he's sure gonna need it messing with you." I hung up on her hoping she wouldn't call back. Just when I thought she was leaving me alone and allowing me to move on with my life she pops back up with more drama. Why can't people just let go and move on with their lives? My cell phone rang three more times and every time I rejected the call, sending it straight to voicemail.

Chapter 18

Charlene

I met up with Mason after running a few errands with Niki so he could go with me to my doctor's appointment. I looked at him as we drove there and noticed that he seemed as if something was bothering him. "Babe you alright?"

Mason snapped out of his daze. "Yeah I'm good, I'm just thinking about you and the twins."

"What about us?"

"I'm just happy that you're having them and I can't wait to get married to you now that my divorce is final." Mason plastered on a smile, but I still felt something was wrong. I figured I'd leave it alone for now though and eventually he'd talk to me when he's ready.

After finishing up at the doctor's office we made our way outside. To my surprise, Ariel was waiting by the door. She approached us with her hands on her hips. "So the bitch really is pregnant." Ariel sucked her teeth as she looked down at my slightly protruding belly with a frown.

"What the fuck are you doing here and how did you know we'd be here?" Mason frowned.

"I followed you here. I got your home address at the divorce proceedings."

"Get the hell out of here we don't need this right now!" Mason shooed her away as if she were a fly.

"I'm not going nowhere, why didn't you tell me she was pregnant? Our divorce just got finalized and you already out here making a family." "Okay and what that got to do with you? It's none of your business what we do."

I was annoyed as hell that she'd have the nerve to stalk and approach us. Where the hell they do that at?

"I wasn't talking to you!" Ariel pointed her finger in my face and I swear it took everything in me not to break it. If it wasn't for me being pregnant I seriously would've hurt her.

"You're talking to my man so you're talking to me." I pushed Ariel's finger out of my face.

"Don't touch me!" She shoved me causing me to stumble back a bit. I immediately reached in my purse for my pepper spray as Ariel moved towards me again but before I could grab it Mason jumped in front of me and shoved her causing her to fall backwards onto the pavement.

"Go home!" Mason glared at Ariel then gently guided me in front of him just in case Ariel tried to run up on me. Ariel ran up just as we got to our car and tried to grab me by my hair. "Bitch this ain't over!" I moved out of the way and swiftly turned around with my pepper spray unlocked. I sprayed a blast of it right in her face. I watched as Ariel screamed and held her face.

"I swear I'm a make you lose them babies!" Ariel yelled at

me through breaths as she continued to cough and wipe away tears from the pepper spray.

"I'd like to see you try!" I aimed another blast of spray towards her eyes. Mason wrapped his arm around my waist and guided me into the car then looked at Ariel and shook his head in disappointment.

"Thank God our divorce is finalized." Mason took one last look at the crowd that formed around us then got in the car and took off, leaving Ariel sitting on the ground wiping her eyes.

I rode home pissed to the point where I didn't even feel like talking. "You alright baby?" Mason looked at me and rubbed my knee.

"Hell no, she's lucky I'm pregnant or I would've happily stomped her face in the ground!"

"Baby calm down. You don't need this kind of stress when you're pregnant."

"No I don't Mason, but tell her that! I'm tired of that bitch trying to cause problems! As a matter of fact, take me to the police station. I'm filing a report and putting a restraining order on her ass." Mason agreed that would probably be a good idea so he turned around and took me to the police station. After we left the police station, I called Niki. "Hey Niki you mind if we come over?"

"No that's fine. You alright?"

"No. Ariel attacked me coming out of the doctor's office."

"Are you serious, are you okay?"

"Yeah I'm fine. I'm just tired of dealing with her. It's just ridiculous that she won't leave us alone. She just doesn't get that it's over between them."

"Don't stress about it. Just make it over here in one piece;

I'll see y'all in a minute."

Niki rushed out to our car when we arrived twenty minutes later. "Did she hurt you or the babies?"

"Nah we're fine. I'm just a little pissed off." Mason and I followed Niki into her house and I immediately went to the living room and plopped down on the couch.

"So what happened?" Niki turned down the TV and sat in a chair across from me.

"That crazy heffa followed us from our house to the doctor's office then tried to fight me after she found out I was pregnant. I knew she wasn't gonna leave us alone."

"You need to file a restraining order against her."

"I did right before I came here. Hopefully she's not stupid enough to break it."

"I don't think that'll be a problem, unless she wants to risk going to jail and losing custody of Nate."

"So what do we do now?"

"We wait and see what happens." Niki got up went to the kitchen and returned with two bottles of water.

"Whose toy is that?" I notice a Barbie doll laying on the floor.

"Oh that's Danielle's. Tanya and her are staying with me for a while."

"I haven't seen her in a minute how is she doing?"

"She's doing alright, just going through some things with Darnelle again."

"I swear she needs to leave that fool." I shook my head.

"Hopefully this time she will cuz Lord knows if she stays she might not live to see another day."

"He's still beating on her huh?"

"Yep and this time it was bad, not saying that the other times were any better. But she was really messed up."

"Dang, I hope she's okay."

"She will be she just needs time to get herself together. Eventually she'll see she'd be better off on her own." Niki and I talked a bit more while Donte and Mason chilled out.

Later on that night after Mason and I got settled into bed I heard Mason's phone ringing. I turned over and saw him glance at it then sit it on the night stand. "It's Ariel again ain't it?"

"Yep, you know how she is."

"Yes and that's the problem." I blew out a frustrated breath and turned back over on my side, facing the wall. After two more rings, Ariel finally got the point and stopped calling so we were finally able to fall asleep. Around two in the morning I got up to use the bathroom and as soon as I finished and returned to bed Mason's phone started ringing again. I looked over at Mason but he was still sleeping so I reached over him and grabbed his phone off the nightstand. Taking one last look at him, I crept out of bed and waddled down the hallway to the guest bedroom. I quietly closed the door behind me and eased down on the bed in the center of the room. I shook my head after seeing Mason had 22 missed calls. This bitch is relentless. The phone began to ring again so I answered it.

"So you finally decided to stop ignoring my calls huh."

"No he didn't, but I did." The line got quiet for a minute.

"Where's Mason I need to talk to him."

"Don't call Mason's phone anymore or I'll report you to the police for harassment."

"Go ahead and do what you gotta do. I'm still gonna keep calling him. And if he keeps ignoring me I'll just show up at his house. I guess you forgot I know where y'all live. He will never get rid of me that easy, I will always be his first lady since I was his first wife." I heard Ariel smirk through the phone.

"Yeah okay keep believing that, that first lady status went down the drain just like your marriage when your divorce got finalized. You're the only one still holding on to old dreams and memories. As for Mason, he's moved on and I'm his family now so you need to do the same because you look real pathetic chasing after a man who no longer wants you. Oh and just a warning, if you do decide to come over my house and start shit I will have your ass put in jail for breaking your restraining order and see to it that you never see your son again."

"Is that a threat?" Ariel asked me.

"I don't know come over my house and see." Ariel got quiet and all I could hear is her breathing into the receiver. Tired of talking I hung up leaving her to talk to the receiver. I said my piece so nothing else needed to be said.

Chapter 19

Tanya

After everything that went down, Mrs. Conway ended up gaining full control of the law firm and immediately asked me to come back. Apparently, because they never signed a prenuptial agreement, she threatened to take all of Mr. Conway's assets so he pretty much gave her whatever she asked for. I hesitated about coming back at first but she offered me a hefty bonus and pay increase that I couldn't refuse. She also apologized profusely for what her husband did to me and promoted me to Head Assistant.

My first day back to work Mrs. Conway greeted me at the door with a hug. "I'm happy you decided to come back after everything that happened."

"Thanks, I'm glad to be back." I sat down at my desk and began unpacking my supplies, and then I heard the front door open. Shelly pranced in and sat down at the desk next to mine.

"May I help you with something?" Mrs. Conway stared at her.

"No, I'm here for work." Shelly continued to check her

emails. Mrs. Conway pulled the plug out the monitor forcing Shelly to look at her.

"Did you not get the memo?"

"What memo?" Shelly looked at her confused.

"The one that stated your services are no longer needed. I emailed it to you."

"Where is Mr. Conway?" Shelly grabbed the phone to call him.

"He's no longer here."

"What do you mean he's no longer here?" Shelly waited on Mr. Conway to pick up the phone but only got his voicemail.

"You're probably not gonna get him, he hasn't answered the phone for anyone since I filed the divorce."

Shelly looked surprised. "So you're finally getting a divorce?"

"Yes ma'am so he's all yours. That is whatever's left of him, because he sure doesn't have much these days."

"He owns this law firm." Shelly smirked.

"I guess you didn't get that memo either huh? I now have sole ownership of this law firm and many other things. He no longer has any say about the company or how its run."

Shelly stood up from her desk folded her arms and began pacing the floor. "I don't believe this."

"Believe it honey. Even if I didn't gain ownership of the law firm did you really think you'd continue to work here after I caught you sleeping with my husband? Honestly, you were fired the moment I found out. Now get your things and leave please." She smirked and pointed to a stack of boxes on the other side of the office. "I was even nice enough to supply those boxes over there in the corner for you." I wanted to laugh, but I just cracked a smile. Shelly finally had gotten what she deserved and I was there to watch the whole thing unfold. I smiled to myself after watching Shelly walk out the door upset and in tears. I had to admit I was having a good day. There's nothing like the feeling of justice.

I began filing papers and looked up to find Darnelle walking through the door, causing my smile to dissipate from my face. "What are you doing here?" I frowned. He was the last person I wanted to see right now.

"I came to see you and apologize. You haven't been home for a while and you wouldn't answer my calls so I figured I could catch you here." The moment Darnelle finished his statement Mrs. Conway walked in the room. "Are you alright Tanya?"

"Yes, I'm ok."

"Are you sure because I'll call the cops if you need me to." Darnelle mean mugged Mrs. Conway but she seemed unfazed.

"No it's fine." I smiled at Mrs. Conway, thankful for her genuine concern.

"Alright yell if you need me." She looked over at Darnelle and pointed in his direction. "I swear if you put one hand on her in my presence I will have you locked up for the rest of your life." She glared at him then walked off.

"I see your boss already knows about me. I wonder who else knows."

"What does it matter, what do you want?"

"I want you and Danielle to come home…"

I looked at him like he had two heads. "Well that's not happening so what else can I do for you?"

"You can't avoid me forever Tanya. Eventually you're

gonna have to come home so we can work this out. We have a daughter together."

"Yeah I know, but you should've thought about that before you put your hands on me."

"Baby I am truly sorry. I didn't mean to hurt you. Please, will you and Danielle come back home?"

"I need time to think because I'll be damned if that happens again. You need to work on your anger issues and seek therapy. Until then, I'm gonna stay right where I am."

"I know baby and I promise I will." Darnelle stood quiet for a minute then looked up at me. "So who are you staying with?"

"Why?" I stared at him annoyed.

"I just wanna know if y'all are safe."

"Believe me we are."

"Tanya I really want to see Danielle. I really miss y'all."

"Now I'll allow you to spend time with Danielle but as far as I'm concerned we're over."

"At least let me try to make it up to you."

"How Darnelle? I still got mental and physical scars I'm trying to get rid of from the day you jumped on me. So how exactly are you gonna make it up to me?" I waited for an answer, but Darnelle just stood there in silence. "Exactly, just what I thought. As I said before I'll bring Danielle by but I'm not staying, just let me know what day you want her to come over."

Darnelle hesitated for a minute. "Alright that's fair, I'll give you a call later on today so we can work something out." He turned to leave but suddenly stopped in his tracks and turned around to look at me. "I know I've hurt you so you have every right to be angry but I really do love you and would like a chance to show you how sorry I am. For now, I will give you a break like you asked but hopefully with time you'll forgive me and let me back in your heart." I watched as he walked out the door but felt pain in my chest from the hurt he's caused. I wanted nothing more than to kiss and make up but I knew things would eventually go right back to the way they were and he would continue to disrespect me. I needed to teach him a lesson and show him I wouldn't stand for being treated as less than what I am and deserve. I must admit though, it felt good to have the upper hand for once. It's too bad I had to get beat down in order to get it.

That evening I picked Danielle up from school and took her to go see a movie then got something to eat. "Mama where's Daddy?" Danielle asked me as she played with the toy that came with her kid's meal.

"He's at work right now honey, his schedule changed so he has to be there more often."

"Are we going to see him again?" Danielle had a sad look on her face.

"Of course we are honey. We're just staying with Aunt Niki because she hasn't spent time with us in a while and she thought it would be fun to have a sleep over. I know you want to see your daddy sweetheart and I promise you will real soon." Danielle was worn out by the time we made it home. She fell asleep in the car so I had to carry her inside and put her to bed. I decided to watch some television and as soon as I got comfortable on the couch I heard a knock on the door. When I opened the door, I was greeted by a tall, fairly handsome man with hazel eyes. "Is Niki home?" The man smiled displaying a set of the prettiest white teeth I'd ever seen.

"No, but how can I help you?"

"I'm James, Shawn's brother. I found out she was getting married so I wanted to come congratulate her and give her this gift. He held up a small box wrapped in gold paper with silver trimming.

"Oh that's kind of you. I can give it to her if you want me to."

"That'll be cool, will you give her this note along with it. She'll know what it's about when she sees it."

"Umm sure, have a nice night." James gave me a head nod then walked off. *Shawn's brother. I knew he looked familiar. I wonder what he wants with Niki.* I sat the gift on the table and held on to the note. Getting comfortable on the couch, I stared at the envelope with the note in it and couldn't help being nosey. I held it up to the light but couldn't see anything so I carefully pulled the tape back, pulled the note out, and unfolded it.

Niki I didn't mean to scare you away or get you in any trouble with Donte. I just wanted you to know how I felt about you. I had no idea Donte would find the letter I wrote you. I would've put it somewhere else or gave it to you personally had I known. I know you love Donte and I tried to respect that by staying away, but when I found out you were getting married to him I lost it. I can't stand by and watch another man marry the woman I want. I love you too much to let that happen without saying or doing something. Now I'm not saying Donte's not a good dude and he may treat you well but I know I can treat you better if you give me the chance. I have a lot more to say to you but I'd rather do it face to face so call me when you get a chance so we can talk. (314) 496-2301. I stared in shock at the letter for a minute but heard somebody pull up in the driveway so I quickly sealed the envelope back up and looked around the living room to find somewhere to hide the gift. Before I could figure out where to put it Niki and Donte walked through the front door.

"Hey Tanya."

"Hey what's up?" Donte looked at the gift box in my hand.

"What's that?"

"What's what?" I nervously shifted from one leg to the other.

"What's that box in your hand?"

"Oh this? Darnelle sent it to me. I guess to make up for what happened."

"He came over here?" Niki frowned. "No, I guess he just mailed it here figuring I was staying with y'all." I stuffed the envelope in my pocket before they could see it thankfully. After asking a few more questions Niki and Donte headed upstairs to get comfortable. Two hours later Niki came back downstairs and took a seat next to me on the couch.

"So why haven't you opened your gift yet?"

"Because it not for me, it's for you." I handed her the box. "I only said it was mine because Donte was with you but some guy named James, who said he was Shawn's brother, dropped it off a while ago. He asked me to give it to you along with this note." I pulled the envelope from my pocket and handed it to Niki. I looked at the frustrated look on Niki's face as she read the note.

"Dammit why won't he just let it go?" She put her face in her hands.

"Did you cheat on Donte with Shawn's brother?"

"No, of course not. I wouldn't cheat on Donte, especially with Shawn's brother. James has had a thing for me ever since we first met but I don't feel the same way. The first time he wrote me one of these letters Donte found it and all hell broke loose. He swore up and down that if he ever saw James again he'd kill him, but of course that never stopped him. James wants what he wants and from the looks of it he won't stop until he gets it. He's a very determined man just like his brother but little does he know you can't always get what you want."

"So how does he know you're getting married?"

"I don't know, I sure didn't tell him. I just hope he doesn't show up at my wedding. The last thing I need is him coming and causing a big commotion."

"Do you think he will?"

"I hope not, but if he's anything like his brother it's a good chance he will. I guess I'll just have to pray on it." Niki sighed.

"I saw he left his number on that note, are you gonna call him?"

"No, if I continue to ignore him maybe he'll go away. I would tell Donte but I don't wanna cause no unnecessary problems."

"Don't worry sis everything will be fine and if not we'll handle it. Now let's see what's in this box. I'd advise you to burn that letter. When we opened the gift box we saw a fuzzy white teddy bear holding a jewelry box with a card that read *To Niki My Love*. In the jewelry box sat a two-carat princess cut diamond ring with a diamond encrusted gold band and engraved inside of it was *Marry Me Niki*.

"Oh my God." Niki and I said in unison as our mouths hang open from shock.

"Niki what are you gonna do?"

"Give it back to him. I can't believe he'd pull a stunt like this! Is he crazy?" Niki continued to stare at the ring.

"Well I guess you better be meeting him because if you keep it you're accepting his proposal."

"What if Donte finds it?" Niki looked at me worried.

"I'll tell him Darnelle gave it to me. It's not like he didn't see the gift box. Hopefully we can get this taken care of before it gets that far."

Chapter 20

Niki

The next morning I woke up a woman on a mission. Donte and I decided to move the wedding date up to August 20, 2013 so I only had five months left of planning to do.

Thankfully, since Tanya's been staying with me I've had extra help. Today I have to meet with my planner and find a way to meet James to handle the engagement ring situation.

Tanya and I went to the bridal shop and checked on the bridesmaids' dresses to see if they had come in yet then we headed over to meet Cynthia, my wedding planner. She greeted us with a hug when we walked in her office then gestured for us to have a seat at her desk. "Alright so we got the venue you wanted for your wedding, but the only dates available are August 16th and the 22nd."

"Okay, we'll take the 22nd."

"Alright I'll let them know." Cynthia smiled. "Now have you made out your guest list yet?"

"Yes, but I'm still juggling some people around."

"Okay, well we're gonna need at least a roundabout

number so we can get a good idea of how many people will be attending."

"Okay." I nodded.

"Now moving on, I have some pictures of four different setups for the wedding. Choose the one you like best and we can go from there unless you have one chosen already." Cynthia handed us the pictures to review. As we scanned them Layla walked in the room.

"Niki, Layla will be ordering the flowers and other materials needed for the wedding, but she will not be assisting me on your wedding day. We want a happy bride." Cynthia added noticing the look on my face. "Is that okay with you? I won't have her to stay if you don't feel comfortable."

"No that's fine as long as she's professional." Layla rolled her eyes at my comment. Thankfully, we got through our meeting with no unnecessary comments or looks so I was happy. Next, I wanted to contact James about his so-called engagement ring. Not wanting him to know my new number, I drove around looking for a pay phone to use to call him. Just my luck I rode around for almost twenty minutes and still hadn't found one. Who would've thought that pay phones would practically be obsolete? What if your cell phone dies or you can't get a signal? Or what if you don't have a cell phone you're just out of luck I guess. Anyway figuring there'd be a pay phone at the metro station, I parked my car and briskly walked inside. *Finally a pay phone.* I sighed with relief. After digging for change, I found two quarters and put them in the coin slot only to have them returned to me. *Great, I finally find a pay phone and it doesn't work, freakin wonderful.* Irritated, I patiently waited for the man using the pay phone next to mine to get off so I could call

James. After holding the phone hostage for like five minutes the man finally got off so I rushed to use it before someone beat me to it.

Hello." James answered after the third ring.

"Hey James, this is Niki. I got the note and gift you brought by the house."

"Did you like it?"

"Yes it was nice. You think we could meet up some time today to talk about it?"

"Yeah, are you busy now?"

"No not really."

"Okay then meet me downtown at the riverfront. Maybe we can grab something to eat."

"Alright, give me about twenty minutes and I'll be there." I was so happy that James agreed to meet me that I practically ran to my car. All I could think about was quickly getting this over with. I spotted James sitting on a bench near the Arch. I walked towards him and he stood to his feet with a schoolboy smile on his face.

"It's nice to see you, you look great." James smiled as he embraced me.

"Thank you, you do too." I smiled not wanting to be rude.

He stared at me for a minute. "Let's grab something to eat. I'm starving." We went to this quiet little sandwich shop he'd been to a couple of times. After ordering our sandwiches, we found a table near the window in the corner of the shop.

"So how'd you like the engagement ring?" James smiled.

"It's nice, but I can't take it. I came here to give it back."

"I get it." James took the ring box from my hand. "It's because I didn't give you a proper proposal." James got out of his seat and knelt down in front of me on one knee then grabbed my hand. "Niki I know you don't know me all that well and I know you dated my brother, but I really want to be with you. I fell in love with you the first day I met you. Being with you would make my life complete so Niki will you marry me? I promise you'll be happy with me if you give me a chance."

"James, get up your embarrassing me." I tried to pull my hand away. "I can't marry you. I love Donte and that's who I'm going to marry."

"Just give me a chance Niki." Suddenly James pulled me into his embrace and kissed me passionately, as I attempted to pull away he held me tighter. When I was finally able to break free I took my right hand and slapped James as hard as I could across his face.

"I don't appreciate you disrespecting me. I've told you I'm marrying Donte so deal with it and move on. I know you don't care that I dated your brother, but I do so I would never date you. Do me a favor and leave me alone." I got up to walk away, but James grabbed my arm.

"I'm not giving up that easy Niki, all I'm asking is for the chance to love you. I'll even come to your wedding if I have to but I'm not giving up without a fight." James let me go and watched me walk off. *How do I always end up with these crazy guys coming after me? What's sad is I didn't even date this one.*

Chapter 21

Ariel

After two weeks of vomiting and feeling nauseous I finally got up the nerve to take the pregnancy test Dana had been bugging me to take. While waiting around for the test results my phone rang. "Hey sorry I haven't called you since the incident. I've been staying with my brother until I find a place because my wife filed for divorce." Keith breathed hard into the phone.

"Why are you breathing so hard?"

"I just finished working out. I called to see if we could meet up tonight."

"I don't know Keith I told you I'm trying to do right by my husband."

"I won't have you out late. I just want to see you for a minute that all."

I hesitated for a minute as I thought about what I should do. "Okay I gotta make a call first then I'll call you back and let you know." After I hang up the phone, I rushed to the bathroom to see the results of the pregnancy test. I examined the test strip and noticed a plus sign. *Oh shit I'm pregnant! What the hell am I going to do now?* Knowing I didn't have many people to turn to I swallowed my pride and called Dana, even though our last conversation didn't go so well.

"Hello." Dana answered on the first ring.

"Hey Dana it's me. I know I'm the last person you want to talk to, but you're practically the only friend that I have."

"That don't sound like no apology to me." Dana snapped at me. "After the way you carried on the last time we spoke you're lucky I even picked up the phone. Then you come to me with this half ass apology? I should hang up on you."

"Look I'm sorry Dana. I really need to talk to you so please don't hang up."

"Humph that's unusual. The words please and sorry never come out your mouth so something seriously got to be wrong. So what's going on?"

"You were right, I took the test and I'm pregnant. I'm staring at the results now."

"Oh damn, what you gonna do?"

"I don't know Dana. I don't know whose baby it is."

"Ariel you gotta tell Mason you cheated. If you tell him now you won't have to worry about it later."

"I don't want this to ruin our marriage." I sighed ready to cry.

"Well get an abortion then you won't have to worry about it anymore."

"I can't Dana. It wouldn't be right."

"It wouldn't be right for you to tell Mason that baby is his when it isn't either so one way or another you're going to have to make a decision. I'm a tell you like this, it's better to get everything out in the open now that way it won't come back to bite you in the butt later. The longer you let this lie linger the worse it's gonna be on you when the truth comes out. Now I'm not trying to tell you what to do, but I just want you to at least take what I've said into consideration."

"I understand all that Dana, but what should I do now?" By this point I had started to get irritated.

"Set up a doctor's appointment to see how far along you are. That way you can get an idea of whose baby it is."

"Okay, I'll set an appointment with my doctor first thing tomorrow morning." After saying that I remembered that I had several appointments scheduled the next day. "Will you let my clients know I'll be in late tomorrow? I'm gonna leave them a message tonight, but just in case they don't get it I need a backup plan."

"Alright I got you. The salon ain't that busy on Thursday's anyway so I'm sure you'll be all right. Call me if you need anything okay."

"Okay, thanks." After hanging up with Dana I made sure I properly disposed of the pregnancy test. I put everything in a separate bag and took it out back to the dumpster. *Now I gotta figure out how I'm gonna tell Mason that I'm pregnant and it's his because there is no way in hell I'm telling him about Keith. Dana's gotta be crazy to think I'm fool enough to do that.*

A couple of hours later Mason walked through the door. "Hey baby what you doing?"

"Nothing just watching TV." I smiled at him as I lay on the sofa.

"Sorry I'm home so late I got caught up in traffic. You

make something eat?"

"No, but I did order takeout. I even got your favorite, pepperoni pizza.

"Cool, come here and give me a hug."

"Okay baby." I walked over to Mason and hugged him tightly while passionately kissing him on the lips. "Baby, I gotta meet up with Dana tonight because I promised I'd go with her to some new lounge she wanted to check out. Is that okay with you because I'll stay home if you want me to?" I looked at him with pleading eyes.

"Go ahead it's cool."

"Are you sure? You can come with us if you want to." Hoping he'd say no, I waited for Mason to answer.

"Nah I'm good. I'm tired so I'm a chill out tonight. Go ahead and have fun."

"Okay baby." I gave him a kiss on the lips, heated his pizza, and then went to change clothes. I was out the door within 20 minutes and heading over to meet Keith. I plugged my earpiece into my phone and called him. "Hey Keith where you wanna meet up?"

"Remember that spot I took you to the night we met?"

"Yeah."

"Meet me there. I'll already be seated when you get there. I knew you'd come."

"How'd you know I was gonna show up? What if I couldn't make it?" I smiled.

"Because I know you and I knew you'd find a way to meet me. I'll see you in a minute."

When I arrived, Keith was already sitting at a table waiting for me just like he'd said.

"Did I keep you waiting long?"

"Nah you good, let me get your seat." As Keith pulled out my chair he glimpsed down at the skirt that rested well above my knees.

"Keith?" I snapped him out of his trance. "Your man let you walk out the house with that on?"

"No I changed on the way here. So what did you want to talk about?"

"Nothing, I just wanted to see you." Keith grinned.

"You know you wrong for that Keith. I could've been at home spending time with my husband."

"Now why would I want that? Clearly he wasn't priority or you wouldn't be here with me." He smiled at me smugly.

After hours of chatting and flirting like two high school kids, Keith and I drove to a park to get out of the public eye. "So did you miss me?" He asked

"Maybe, maybe not?" I flirted.

"Okay I'm a ask you again, did you miss me?" Keith slid his hand under my skirt while kissing my neck.

"I don't know."

"You don't know? Why you don't know?" Keith whispered in my ear then instructed me to get in the backseat of his car. Climbing on top of me he passionately kissed my lips as he teased me with his fingers under my skirt. "Did you miss me baby?" Keith whispered in my ear again.

"Yes Keith, yes." I cooed through labored breaths. Yearning for more we grinded against each other uncontrollably. "Please give it to me." I begged Keith.

"Yes baby." Keith fulfilled my every desire and then some. Exhausted we laid in the back seat for a while.

"Baby what time is it?" I asked Keith while scrambling for my phone. After retrieving it, I noticed I had three missed calls. One was from Dana and the other two from Mason. I got out of the car and frantically dialed Mason's number. I put my finger up to my lips as a gesture for Keith to be quiet. "Hello." Mason answered groggily.

"Hey baby I'm sorry I'm calling back so late, I didn't hear my phone ring. Dana caught a flat tire on the highway so we had to wait on the insurance company to come and assist with putting it on."

"I thought y'all rode in separate cars."

"No I left my car at her house. We figured it would be pointless to take two cars, plus it would save us gas."

"You mean to tell me neither of y'all know how to change a tire?"

"No Mason, please don't be mad. We just didn't want some random stranger helping us seeing how it's so late. I would've called you, but I thought you might be sleep and I didn't want to wake you."

"I ain't mad baby I just want you to make it home safely. So what's going on now? Did they change the tire yet?"

"Yeah, I'm on my way home now so I should be there in a minute. We just had to stop by her house so I could get my car."

"Alright baby, I'll see you when you get home and call me if you need me." I hopped back to the car relieved when Mason hung up.

"Everything good?"

"Yeah I'm good. I told him I'd be home in a minute so I gotta go." Keith walked me over to my car and hugged me tightly as we kissed.

"Am I gonna see you again?"

"I don't know Keith we'll see." The answer was most likely no, but I didn't want to get into a debate about it so I conjured up the best response I could. After I left Keith, I pulled over to a 24 hour McDonald's and changed clothes in the bathroom. Somehow, I would have to take a shower tonight without looking suspicious. First thing tomorrow morning I'm changing my cell phone number so Keith can't call me no more. I never told Dana that Mason caught me cheating once before. He said if it happened again we're through. I would do whatever I had to do to make sure that he never found out about Keith and I. So far as I'm concerned, Keith never happened and this is his child no questions asked.

When I got home I claimed to smell like cigarette smoke. I had rehearsed that lie in my car the entire ride home. As soon as I told Mason, I headed straight to the shower to wash off Keith's scent.

When I lay down in bed Mason began caressing my thigh. "I missed you baby." He whispered in my ear as he slowly climbed on top of me. I knew I couldn't refuse him without him suspecting something so I let him have his way without a protest.

The next morning I woke up feeling sicker than I had in the two weeks prior. I hopped out of the bed, ran to the bathroom, and scrambled over to the toilet. I felt completely miserable and could barely lift my head out of the toilet. Concerned, Mason walked in behind me. "You alright baby?"

"I don't know. I think I got the flu." As I struggled to stand up my knees buckled underneath me. Mason caught me in his arms.

"That's it. I'm taking you to the hospital."

"Mason you can't miss work."

"Don't worry about that. Let me help you get dressed." Mason escorted me back to the bedroom.

"Don't take me to the hospital. I already set up a doctor's appointment for this morning. I sensed I was coming down with something so I called ahead of time." When we arrived at the doctor's office Mason sat me down in a chair and filled out a patient information form for me. Fifteen minutes later a nurse in SpongeBob scrubs called me to the back office. She took my vital signs and escorted me to a room while Mason waited up front for me in the waiting room. The nurse handed me a paper gown and told me to get undressed and that the doctor would be with me in one minute. "Good morning Mrs. Clark." The doctor smiled as he entered the room. "So what's the reason for your visit today?"

"I haven't been feeling all that well."

"What issues are you having?" I told the doctor the various symptoms that I had been experiencing and he concluded that I may be pregnant, which I already knew of course. He gave me a physical examination and had me urinate and in a cup. Ten minutes later the doctor was back with my results. "Yep you're definitely pregnant."

"So would you like me to bring your husband in?"

"Sure."

Feeling nervous, I knew this was my only option. I just couldn't tell Mason the truth. I had too much to lose. A couple of minutes later the doctor returned with Mason. "Is everything okay Doctor?"

"Yes, have a seat please." The doctor gestured with his hands. "I called you in here to inform you that your wife is pregnant.

"She's... huh?" Mason looked at me shocked.

"Your wife is about three weeks pregnant."

"She is?" Mason looked at me again then smiled. "I'm gonna be a daddy!" Excited, Mason grabbed me and hugged me tight. Noticing the worried look on my face Mason assured me that everything would be fine and that he'd be here to help me. That was only the beginning of my big lie. He was so excited about the baby that I couldn't break his heart. He loved Nate with all his heart and I didn't want to be responsible for ruining that.

Now here it is eight years later and I've lost everything. I even lost my friendship with Dana. When Nate was about two years old, Dana called me as usual to talk some sense into me. "Hey girl, you tell him yet?" Dana would ask only to get the same answer.

"No I haven't got around to it."

"Ariel you've been saying that for two years now. You're never going to tell that man. He shouldn't be responsible for a child that isn't his."

"Who said it isn't his? It very well could be so I don't see no point of digging up the past." Irritated, I rubbed my hand down my face.

"You ain't right Ariel. I don't know how you could even sleep at night knowing what you've done."

"Dana, don't give me that self-righteous bullshit you've

done your dirt to!"

"Yeah but at least I own up to it, maybe you should take a page out of my book. You're playing with people's lives and it ain't right. Mason and Nate both deserve to know who that boy's real father is!"

"Dana I'm tired of you trying to tell me how to run my life. This is my decision and you have nothing to do with it so stay the hell out of my business!"

"Stay the hell out of your business? You weren't saying that every time you called me crying about your troubles with Mason and your pregnancy. You were dishing it all out then! You aren't the only one who should be making the choice about Nate's father and you're going to cause Mason and Nate to suffer over your silly mistake. Be a woman and take responsibility for what you've done!"

"Bitch please, who are you to tell me anything you don't even have a man. So you can't tell me shit!"

"Oh I'm a bitch now? First off, I do have a man who I've been with for almost two years now. Of course, you wouldn't know that because you were so engulfed in your own problems that I could never tell you what was going on with me. Two, I'm not the one whose life is going to fall apart because I'm too afraid to admit the truth. Yours is. And since you want to call names, our friendship is over. I'm just going to leave you with these last few words though, what's done in the dark eventually comes to light. I refuse to stand by and watch a good man get hurt because of your hoe tendencies so get ready for a rude awakening." Dana slammed the phone down leaving me stuck listening to the dial tone. That's the day my best friend became my worst enemy.

A month after we stopped talking Dana called Mason and told him it would be wise for him to get a DNA test because there was a good chance that Nate might not be his. From that point on Mason never trusted me again and constantly mentioned having a paternity test done. I did everything I could to convince him otherwise but he wasn't having it.

One night after Nate was born, I came home late after hanging out at the club. We had to be at the club by ten o'clock to get in free so I left the spare house key under the mat on the front porch for the babysitter and left but I forgot to see if the babysitter arrived for Nate. Before I left to hangout I called her and she said she was five minutes away so figuring he'd be okay, I made sure Nate was asleep then headed out to meet my friends.. I never thought for one minute that the babysitter would have car trouble and be stranded on the highway. When I made it back home Mason was livid. "Bitch are you crazy!" Mason yelled as I walked through the door.

"You're out gallivanting in the streets looking like a hoe while our son is here home alone!"

I looked at him sideways. "What do you mean, he had a babysitter!"

"Had you answered your phone you would've known she couldn't make it! Luckily the babysitter got in contact with our neighbors after she called me and they were nice enough to watch him until I made it home!"

"Well there, problem solved!"

"I swear I wish I never met your simple ass. You're an unfit mother and wife and I think it will be in our best interest to separate for a while because if I don't I might kill you." Mason stared at me while pacing back and forth across the floor while trying to calm himself down. "And since you can't be a mother I'm sending Nate to stay with my parents until I decide what I want to do. If you want to see him you can do it on the days he's staying with your mother."

"You can't do that!"

"Watch me, already called your parents and mine to set everything up. They both agree this would be best for Nate."

"So you're just gonna leave me and take my son!"

"You're lucky no one called child protective services because then the state would have him!" Without saying another word Mason went upstairs and packed some of his and Nate's things.

"Please don't leave Mason. I promise I'll do better."

"Please, you had seven years to do better and you still haven't changed so I'm not trying to hear that."

"But Mason…"

"Let me go Ariel." Mason jerked his arm away from me.

"Give me my son, you're not taking him!" I pulled Nate away from Mason by his arm.

"What are you doing? Are you trying to hurt him! This is not a game of tug-of-war he's a human being." Mason stared at me as if I was crazy. Before I could respond, there was a knock on the door.

"How could you put that boy's life in jeopardy the way you did have you lost your mind!" My mother yelled at me as she stormed through the door. "I didn't raise you to be some half ass mother!"

"I didn't know the babysitter wasn't going to show up!" I

tried to defend myself.

"You didn't wait around to see either now did you! You so busy out clubbing that you forgot about your son's safety!"

"Don't chastise me Mama! I'm a grown woman!" The next thing I know my mother slapped me so hard my cheek went numb.

"Don't you raise your voice at me girl. I don't care how grown you think you are you're going to show me some respect!" She pointed her finger in my face. "You were wrong for leaving that boy here by himself and if Mason left you I honestly wouldn't blame him." Brushing past me my mother went upstairs to get Nate and his things. When she came back downstairs she turned to Mason and said, "I'm sorry about all this Mason. I hope everything works out okay."

"Thank you Ms. Davis." Mason hugged her.

She looked at Mason sympathetically. "I'm gonna drop him off over your parent's house in the morning since it's so late. I'll see you later Mason." My mother looked at me with disgust and walked by me without uttering another word. I couldn't believe my own mother was treating me this way.

By the time I closed the door behind my mother Mason had gone upstairs to start packing. Angry, I stormed upstairs and asked, "Why didn't you tell me she was coming over here?"

"Why are you such a shitty mother?" Mason frowned then grabbed his bags. "I'll let you know my decision in two weeks." He stormed past me and headed downstairs so I followed him.

"Your decision about what?"

"Getting a divorce." Then he slammed the door behind him leaving me standing in the middle of the floor looking dumbfounded. That's when I knew I really messed up. I lost my whole family in one night and was it worth it just to go to the club?

Chapter 22

Candy

Taye and I hit it off pretty well. He had gone above and beyond to make sure SJ and I were comfortable. I asked him almost a hundred times what I could do in return to say thank you and he'd always tell me to find a new job and take care of SJ.

"Where you going?" Taye asked me as I grabbed my purse. "I have to go to work."

"Well I'm getting ready to head up there too so do you wanna ride with me?"

"Sure, but how am I gonna get home?"

"I'll bring you home. I gotta help my uncle out with some stuff in the office so I'll probably be there for a while." When we arrived at the club it was packed as usual. Lucky for me I only had to dance twice tonight because I really didn't feel like being bothered. My first dance of the night went pretty well, the men behaved themselves and tipped nicely. Now the second dance was a whole other story. I danced around the stage like a Las Vegas showgirl teasing the crowd of men as I swung around on the pole like a pro. Mastering the art of seduction I gracefully made my way to the front of the stage, dropped down into a full split, and began grinding my hips into the floor. Face to face with one of the men who stood in front stage, I turned around and spread my legs apart allowing him to sneak a peek at the treasure he longed to see. The man grinned then tugged at the crotch of my thong to place a 20-dollar bill inside. Pleased with his tip I gave the man a wink and moved on to the next patron who dared to test my skills. Crawling on my hands and knees, I eased over to a handsome fella who appeared to be mixed with Hispanic and Black that was standing at the end of the stage. I rubbed my hands through his curly hair and stared into his almond shaped eyes. As I dropped down into a Chinese split in front of him he placed a 10-dollar bill in the crack of my thong without saying a word. He slightly grazed my thigh then suddenly climbed up on stage like a wild man and grabbed me. He practically ripped off my thong and bikini top as he attempted to kiss my neck and body while fondling whatever body parts he could get his hands on first. While I screamed for help and attempted to push him off of me I watched thirsty men look on lustfully as if they too wanted to participate.

Just when I thought no one would help me I saw a familiar face darting through the crowd as security rushed behind him. "Taye!" I screamed happy to see his face. He leapt up on stage and snatched the man off me then punched him in his mouth, splitting his lip. As the man stumbled backward and held his mouth Taye rushed him delivering blow after blow to his face, ribs, and abdomen until security pulled him off of the guy. Security dragged the beaten and bloody man off stage and took him outside where they finished the brutal beat down.

"You alright?" Taye covered me up with his jacket and walked me off stage.

"Yes now that you're here. I don't know what would've happened if you hadn't come."

"I'm sorry about what happened to you. That usually doesn't happen here most of the men are usually well behaved." Taye looked at me sympathetically.

"I'm a little shaken up, but I'll be okay."

"Are you sure because you don't look okay." I buried my head in Taye's chest and softly cried. Taye held me tight and softly caressed my hair.

"It's alright. I'm not going to let anything happen to you."

I looked up into Taye's eyes and gently kissed his lips; he kissed me back and held me even tighter than before. "Don't worry I got you." Taye whispered to me. That night when we got home things were different, Taye was no longer the insensitive jerk I met in the club anymore. He had become a friend or possibly more if he wanted to be. He was caring, confident, and strong. Which was everything I needed and wanted in a man. "How you feeling?" Taye sat next to me on my bed.

"I'm good thank you for being there for me. I have never had any one treat me the way you do."

"That's because I'm one-of-a-kind." Taye grinned causing me to smile. "My aunt told me to tell you SJ's fine and she appreciates you letting him stay the night."

"Oh it's no problem I appreciate the help." I began thinking about everything that took place and how Taye was always there to help me when I needed him.

"Why you so quiet?"

"I was just thinking about how different you are from other men I've met. I thought you were a jerk at first, but you're nothing like that."

"Okay thanks, if that's a compliment." Taye laughed lightly. "You're not like most of the strippers I've met either. I can tell in your heart you want to do better, but you're afraid of failing so you stick to what you know. I'm going to change that though, hopefully what happened tonight will be a wake-up call for you and make it easier for you to let me help you. You raised a good kid. I'd hate to see something happen to you and you not be able to be there for him. True enough stripping may get you good money, but it can be a dangerous job." He caressed my face and softly kissed me on my forehead. I moved closer to him and kissed his lips as he held my face in his hands.

"I like how it feels when you touch me."

"I like touching you." Taye smiled then laid me back on the bed. We took things a step further as our bodies intertwined in a heat of passion and for the first time in my life I experienced how it felt to make love. As I lay on his chest dozing off to sleep, I thought to myself, *Is this love and if it is I hope it isn't one-sided.* I've had men come in and out of my life like a whirlwind using me for their own gain then tossing me aside. For this reason, I vowed never to get close to another man again, but now I don't know. Taye might be the one to change all that.

Chapter 23

Tanya

Darnelle finally called a week after he came my job to set up arrangements to see Danielle. I rushed from work to pick up Danielle from school and drop her off with him at the agreed time. "Come on and get in the car honey Daddy's waiting on us." Danielle ran to the car and I quickly strapped her in her car seat so we could leave. When we made it in front of the house Darnelle was already there waiting.

"Have you been waiting long?" I asked him while helping Danielle out the car.

"Nah, I got here right before you did."

"Here are Danielle's clothes. There should be enough in there for two weeks. If not, she still has clothes here." I handed Darnelle a black duffel bag. "Come give Mommy a hug and a kiss." I knelt down to Danielle's height. "I'll be back to get you in a couple weeks okay." I smiled as I caressed her cheek. She gave me one more hug then I turned to walk away but Darnelle grabbed my arm and pulled me into him.

"I'm sorry baby. Please come home?" He asked then gently kissed my lips.

"I can't. I'm sorry." I tried to pull away, but he held me tighter.

"Please."

"Darnelle I can't. I'm not ready."

He stared at me like he was deep in thought. "Okay how about this, when you come back to get Danielle maybe we can do something together if you're okay with that."

I hesitated for a minute. "I guess that'll be okay."

Darnelle smiled. "Alright baby be careful going home and if you don't mind, call me when you get there so I'll know you made it okay." I nodded my head then got in the car to leave. As I drove home, I stared at the road lost in thought. I know I said I didn't want Darnelle anymore, but I love him and maybe the time I've spent away from him has made him change. True enough he can't change overnight, but he at least seems to be trying.

Two weeks later when I returned to pick up Danielle he told me that he had taken her to my mother's house. "Why isn't she here?" I glared at him.

"Because I wanted to take you out. You're mother agreed to watch her until we get back." He eyeballed my work clothes and raised his eyebrows. "Is that what you're wearing?"

"No, I should have something to wear in the house. I didn't take everything when I left."

Darnelle took a seat on the couch and told me to take my time getting ready. I came downstairs thirty minutes later in a black fitted dress with a plunging neckline that showed just enough cleavage and rested just above my knees. I topped it off with a pair of red stilettos that strapped around my ankle. I twirled around to show off my dress and asked, "You ready to go?"

Darnelle stared at me with approval. "Now that's more like it." That night he took me to see a movie and then out to dinner, and to my surprise we had a great time. He even held my hand, opened doors, and pulled out chairs for me throughout the night, which was rare. For the first time in a long time we laughed and joked like two high school kids reminding me of when we first met. It often makes me wonder when things changed.

After that night, Darnelle and I began going out on a regular basis. We'd go to the movies, out to eat, and sometimes even bowling, which he hated. Darnelle was now more caring and spontaneous, that was something he'd never been before. Viewing things in a more positive light, I decided to move back home. Niki and Mrs. Conway weren't too thrilled with my decision and felt I was making a big mistake, but I finally felt like we were the family we once were in the past. Happy that I decided to come back home, Darnelle took Danielle and I out to eat and promised that things would be better from now on.

It's now three months later and to my surprise I haven't had any more incidents of Darnelle abusing me verbally or physically. It's as if he's a different man. He's kept every promise he made to me. "How you feeling this morning baby?" Darnelle hugged me and kissed me on the forehead as I fixed a plate of biscuits, eggs, and bacon for him and Danielle.

"I'm good, where you going?" I asked after noticing he was fully dressed.

"I got called into work, but I should be home by three."

"Are we still going to the movies later?"

"Yeah, we'll catch the five o'clock show." As I opened the refrigerator to grab a carton of orange juice I began to feel woozy and lost my balance. Darnelle caught me from behind and eased me down in a chair. "Are you okay baby?

"I don't know. I feel lightheaded."

"Are you hungry? Maybe you need to eat something." Darnelle put his hand on my forehead. "You don't have a fever." Darnelle sat a plate of food in front of me and poured me a glass of juice. "Here, why don't you try to eat something then lay down for a minute?"

"I gotta take Danielle to school." I protested.

"Don't worry about that, I'll take her. Just get some rest."

After finishing breakfast, Darnelle helped Danielle gather her things together for school then gave me a hug and a kiss. "I have to get ready to go but if you start feeling any worse call me and I'll come home."

"Okay." I smiled as he headed out the door. Once they left I threw on a jogging suit and headed to the store to purchase a pregnancy test. I had been feeling sick for the past week, but I didn't want to tell Darnelle until I got the test results. I was back at home twenty minutes later waiting around for the results of the test. I raced back to the bathroom after putting on a pot of tea and picked up the test stick. It displayed two lines. *Great. I'm pregnant.* I didn't know whether to be happy or sad, true enough Darnelle appeared to be different, but who knows how he's gonna react when I tell him this. The anticipation of Darnelle coming home was driving me nuts, I felt like I had been waiting an eternity for him to get here. All I could do was sit around and watch the clock as my nerves turned into balls of knots that twirled around in my stomach. *Two more hours.* I looked at the clock on the wall and rehearsed how I planned to break the news to him. As I began to doze off to sleep on the couch I heard the front door unlock.

"Hey baby you feeling any better?"

"Yeah a little, where's Danielle?"

"Your mother's going to pick her up from school and drop her off later."

"Oh okay." *It's now or never.* "Darnelle, I need to talk to you about something."

Darnelle looked at me worried. "Is everything alright?"

"Yes, but I have something I need to tell you." Darnelle sat down on the couch next to me.

"Ok shoot."

I turned to face him. "Darnelle I'm pregnant." Not knowing what to say he sat and stared at me in silence.

He finally spoke again after collecting his thoughts. "Are you sure?"

"Yes, I took a home pregnancy test earlier while you were at work."

"Do you want to keep it?" Darnelle nervously rubbed his forehead.

"I would like to." He leaned back on the couch and looked at me again.

"Well, I guess I'm a be a daddy then." He smiled. Relieved I wrapped my arms around his neck and hugged him tight. "I gotta go call Niki." I leaped up off the couch and raced to the phone.

"Guess what Niki? I'm going to have a baby!" I barely allowed her time to speak before telling her the news.

"You're what? When did this happen?" Niki sounded

confused.

"I found out earlier today."

"Have you told Darnelle yet?"

"Yes and he's happy about it." I beamed.

"Well congratulations... I guess."

"Why'd you say it like that? You don't sound happy for me." I heard Niki sigh.

"Tanya I'm not trying to be funny, but I'm not. This is the same dude that beat the hell out of you just a few months ago. Taking that into consideration do you really want to have another kid by him?"

"Niki, he is my husband. Besides that he's been fine lately and our relationship's been great so I don't see the problem."

"The problem is he could change up at any moment. Just because he's being cool now doesn't mean he's going to stay that way. Darnelle is controlling and wants everything his way so the first time y'all get into another disagreement he's gonna hit you again."

"That was one time Niki."

"Please Tanya that was not the first time he put his hands on you. That man is like a ticking time bomb waiting to explode so you better believe it's gonna happen again."

I began to get annoyed. "Whatever Niki you're just jealous!"

"Of what Tanya? Your abusive ass husband, not at all. I'm just trying to be real with you. He may really hurt you one day and I don't want to see that happen."

"It amazes me how you're always so critical of me. It's like you're never just happy for me."

"I'd be happy for you if Darnelle wasn't such a jerk. If you saw what I saw when you came to my house all beat up that day you wouldn't like him either... I'm not gonna sit here and argue with you though, if that's what you want to do by all means do it. I just know that it feels a lot better not having to sleep with a gun under your pillow and one eye open because the man, who claims to love you, got you scared."

"He does love me and he's trying to do better."

"Trying isn't good enough Tanya. You deserve better and don't need that type of drama in your life, especially with Danielle around."

"I understand that Niki, but he promised he'd change and things are going to be better, which they have." I tried to sound hopeful.

"Believe what you want, but it's highly unlikely that he's gonna change that quick... Anyway, I love you and I'll always be here for you so if you want to keep this baby I'm behind you 100 percent. All I'm asking you is to not be so naïve to think it could never happen again and get comfortable. Always keep your guards up, the police on speed dial, and that gun close because you'll never know when you might have to use it."

Thinking about what she said I sighed. "Niki I hope I never have to use it."

"I hope you don't either Tanya. But with us going to the gun range and all, at least you know how to use it if you need to." We talked a bit about Niki's wedding and then we hung up so I headed upstairs to the bedroom.

Darnelle had the curtains closed and was lying down so figuring he decided to take a nap I went to go lay down beside him.

He startled me when he asked, "So what happened with Niki?"

"Nothing we talked a little bit about the wedding."

"What'd she say about the baby?"

"Oh nothing much, she was worried about me not having the finances to take on another child."

"Why's she worried about that? I'm here, it's not like you're going to be by yourself."

"I guess just in case anything happens she wants me to be able to manage on my own."

"See that's why I don't like you talking to her ass because she starts putting all these silly ideas in your head."

Darnelle and Niki had never seen eye to eye so she only comes around occasionally because she doesn't like to be around him. As for Darnelle, he's always felt like she was the one person who could end our marriage given the right ammunition so he never likes me talking to her long. "She wasn't trying to put anything in my head, she was just saying…"

"She was just saying what Tanya? I ain't gonna be around?"

"She didn't say that Darnelle. Why do you have to make everything into an argument?"

"Because your ignorant ass family always got something to say. You think I don't know they dislike me? I know they don't like me, but they ain't gonna keep saying shit about me behind my back!"

"What are you talking about Darnelle? Ain't nobody said nothing about you and my family ain't ignorant."

"I ain't trying to hear that shit Tanya. I heard y'all talking about me."

"You're eavesdropping on my conversations now?" Before he could reply, the doorbell rang so he jumped out of bed and ran downstairs.

"Who is it?" Darnelle snatched the door open before anyone could reply.

"Oh hey Mrs. Whitfield."

"Hey Darnelle, I just came to drop Danielle off. Is everything alright?" She asked noticing the look on Darnelle's face.

"Yeah everything's good. I'm just a little tired that's all."

"Alright then get some rest and call me if y'all need anything."

"Thanks Mrs. Whitfield." Darnelle closed the door behind her, grabbed Danielle by the hand, and escorted her to her room. "Time to take a nap."

"But Daddy I'm not tired."

"I don't want to hear it Danielle. Just do what I said."

Darnelle was fuming with anger. He stormed out of the room and slammed the door behind him. He walked down the hallway to the bedroom and began pacing the floor in thought. "Tanya I don't want your sister calling here no more."

I looked at him as if he had two heads. "Excuse me, as long as she's my sister she has the right to call this house."

"I will not stand for your sister calling here disrespecting me."

"Whatever Darnelle. I'm not going to sit here and argue with you about something that's not gonna change. I am not telling Niki she can't call here no more. It's bad enough I barely get to see her so that's not happening." I waved him off and walked out the room but he followed behind me and grabbed my arm. "Do not

218

grab me." I stared him down as if he'd lost his mind.

"I'm not finished talking to you."

"It doesn't matter Darnelle I am." I snatched my arm away and pushed him out of my way.

"Where are you going?"

"I'm sleeping in the guest bedroom. We will not have another incident like last time because this time I might actually hurt you." I said with confidence and strutted down the hall. Darnelle stormed back in the bedroom and slammed the door while I continued downstairs to the guest bedroom. I grabbed an extra pillow and blanket out of the closet, lay across the bed, and flicked on the TV. *How dare he tell me I can't talk to my sister anymore? That fool has lost his mind.*

As I watched TV, my stomach began growling so I headed to the kitchen for a snack. *Humm what do we have?* I rummaged through the refrigerator. I made a sandwich, grabbed a drink and a cup of yogurt, and then turned to head back to the room but Darnelle was standing right in front of me. I was so startled that I dropped my drink. "Are you coming back upstairs?"

"No I'm sleeping down here." I mopped up the drink I spilled as he stood and stared at me.

"I want you to come back upstairs." He grabbed my hand forcefully and tried to pull me towards the stairs but I refused to go and snatched away.

"Dammit why can't you just leave me alone? I don't want to be around you right now." I walked towards the room and tried to close the door but he stuck his foot in it so it wouldn't close.

"Don't walk away from me when I'm talking to you."

"The last time I checked I'm a grown ass woman so if I

want to sleep down here that's my decision to make not yours." He grabbed me by my shirt and shoved me across the room causing everything I was holding to fly forward and hit the floor. "Look what you did! What the fuck is your problem Darnelle?"

"Your mouth, that's my problem! You're not gonna keep talking to me all crazy."

"You came here and started bothering me. It wasn't the other way around!"

"Whatever. Pick that shit up and come upstairs!"

"No, I don't want to be bothered with you right now and I'm not going to." He reached out to grab me again, but I pushed him out the door. "Don't touch me!" I watched his facial expression change into something demonic so I quickly closed the door and locked it so he couldn't get back in.

"Open the door Tanya." He pulled at the handle, but the door wouldn't budge. "I ain't playing with you. Open this damn door before I kick it in!" He continued to beat on the door, but I refused to open it. I was Afraid of what Darnelle might do so I grabbed my cell phone and called the police then I dialed Niki's number right after.

"Hey, you alright?" Niki asked me as if she sensed something was wrong.

"No. You are right Niki he hasn't changed."

"What's going on? I hear him yelling in the background!"

"He's trying to break down the door Niki. I don't know what to do I'm scared." I whispered into the receiver as I hid in the corner of the room.

"Did you call the cops yet?"

"Yes, right before I called you."

"Good now if you gotta shoot his ass at least you'll be covered. Now where is your gun?"

"In my room, but I'm downstairs in the guest bedroom."

"Can you get pass Darnelle to get it?"

"I doubt it."

Suddenly, Darnelle burst through the door, stormed over to me, and grabbed me by my hair. "I ain't gonna keep playing these games with you!" He dragged me out the room.

I clutched my phone in my hand and began pleading for Niki to help me. "I'm coming Tanya! I'm coming!" Niki yelled through the receiver hoping I could hear her.

"Who the fuck you talking to?" Darnelle snatched the phone out my hand and threw it against the wall causing it to shatter into pieces. "Who were you talking to Tanya? It was some dude wasn't it? That's probably who you were with the day you disappeared. That's why I fucked you up that day because I knew you were lying. Is that where you and Danielle were staying when you left for that minute? Tell the truth, that baby ain't mine either is it?" Darnelle barraged me with a bunch of questions.

"I didn't lie to you. I wasn't with no dude!" I tried to pry his hands off my head.

"Man please. All of a sudden you pop up pregnant... you was probably waiting for the right time to tell me thinking I'd fall for it. That's what you was talking to your sister on the phone about, I ain't stupid." He finally let go of my hair.

"I ain't messing with no dude Darnelle!"

"Who was you talking to then?"

"Niki!"

"You lying! You wasn't talking to Niki that's why you was

trying to sleep in the guest room so you could sneak and talk to ole boy!"

I knew I had to do something soon when I noticed the evil glare in Darnelle's eyes so I pulled myself off the floor and attempted to run past him. I made it to the top of the stairs and ran down the hall and towards the bedroom. That's when I felt my legs fly from underneath me and I fell forward. When I turned over and looked up Darnelle was standing over me with a sadistic expression on his face. He got on top of me and slapped me in the face as hard as he could, causing me to hold my jaw. "Who were you talking to?"

"I already told you I was talking to Niki." I mumbled through tears.

"Wrong again." Darnelle yanked my hands down to the side and put his knees on my wrist so I couldn't block the next blow. Overpowered and out of breath I watched in horror as he raised his hand to hit me again, but Danielle came out of her room and ran towards us.

"Get off of my mommy!" Danielle pounded her tiny fist on Darnelle's back in an attempt to help me. Agitated, Darnelle grabbed Danielle by her shirt and shoved her into the wall. At that moment, I wiggled from underneath him and darted down the hall to the bedroom. I rushed to the closet, reached in my shoebox, grabbed my gun and ran back into the hallway.

"Get away from my daughter!" I pointed the gun at Darnelle.

"What you gonna do with that? Shoot me?"

"Try me and you'll see." With a stern look on my face, I dared him to come any closer to Danielle or me. "Put the gun down Tanya. You and I both know you're not gonna use it."

"I will if I have to. Now get out the way so me and Danielle can leave." While still pointing the gun at him, I made my way over to Danielle. She was laying on the floor and didn't make a sound. "What did you do to my baby?" I wiped away tears as I checked to see if she was still breathing. "Come on sweetie wake up." I heard a slight groan escape her mouth and I grabbed her and held her tightly. "Everything's going to be okay baby Mama's here."

I noticed Darnelle creeping forward I let out a warning shot towards his feet. "I said stay where you are. If you move again the next time I won't miss." I continued to aim the gun at him and he backed up with his hands in surrender.

"Alright you got it."

I turned my attention back to Danielle and attempted to pick her up off the floor. Before I could pick her up completely, felt a hard shove in my back that caused me to drop Danielle back to the floor. I fell forward and the gun slid across the hallway. Darnelle and I both darted for the gun. Though I was ahead of him, I felt Darnelle behind me. He grabbed my shirt and pulled me backwards as I attempted to shove him causing both of us to stumble to the floor. "Let me go!" I bit Darnelle on the arm and he yelled out in pain. I then attempted to reach the gun, but he kicked me in the side. I screamed from the pain and held my ribs, but still scrambled to reach the gun.

Just as I got my hand on the handle, Darnelle grabbed me and tried to wrestle it out of my hand. I felt the gun slipping so I tried to maintain my grip, but my hand was still on the trigger. "Let go Darnelle!" He put his hand around my throat and tried to pry the gun away from me with the other. Before I could move my hand away, the trigger slipped, shooting him in the stomach. "Darnelle?" I stared at him as he rolled off me and landed on his back facing the ceiling. He held his stomach and grimaced in pain. "I'm sorry I didn't mean to." I crawled over to his side and watched him squirm as I put pressure on his stomach with my hand in an attempt to slow down the bleeding. "I was gonna shoot you in the leg or arm nowhere that would kill you. I only wanted you to back off. Why couldn't you just leave us alone and let us go?" I looked down at him through teary eyes. "I really didn't mean for this to happen."

He put his finger up to my lips to shush me and tried to speak as sirens blared in the background and someone pounded on the front door. "It's... okay. I... never meant... to hurt...you or Danielle." He said to me through labored breaths. "Promise me... you'll take care of... Danielle."

"I will. I promise." I stared down at him and he reached up and caressed my face. "I'm s... sorry for everything... I love you." I saw a single tear roll down his cheek then his face went blank and his once tight grip on my hand loosened.

"Darnelle!" I shook him, but got no response. Stuck in a daze I sat on the floor horrified with tears streaming down my cheeks as I watched the man I loved gasp and take his last breath. I stared at his lifeless body for a moment before I slowly closed his eyes and then scooted over towards Danielle. Suddenly, I heard the front door burst open.

"Tanya!" I heard Niki yelling frantically as she rushed upstairs with the cops behind her.

"Oh my God!" Niki ran over to Danielle and I, who was

now conscious.

"An ambulance should be here in a minute." One of the cops reassured me. As I sat staring off in space, all I could think about was how my life had crumbled in such a short period of time. I wondered if I would ever be able to pick up the broken pieces that were left and put them back together again.

Chapter 24

Candy

The past few months have been great, Taye is wonderful to SJ and I and I'm glad to have found him. He's been here for SJ and I like no one ever has and for that I'm grateful, but like all good things it must come to an end. I still remember the day I told Shawn about our new living arrangements and of course, he was livid. Now every time I go to visit him I get an earful of nonsense. "You got another man around my child playing daddy. How am I supposed to feel Candy, of course I'm not going to be happy." Shawn complained through the phone as we sat in a booth that separated us with a Plexiglas window.

"Shawn it's only temporary. We needed a place to stay and Taye offered us one. It's not like you could help us seeing how you're here in prison. Taye was nice enough to take us in so you could at least be appreciative."

"Get the fuck outta here with that shit. I ain't gonna be appreciative of y'all staying with some random ass dude you just met. You barely even know this fool."

"Shawn it amazes me how you always have so much to say

about the decisions I make but you can't do anything to help us. Besides I didn't come here to get confirmation about our living arrangements from you, I came here so you could see your son."

"I don't want my son around that dude so y'all are gonna have to move."

I laughed lightly at Shawn's demand. "You're not calling any shots. Especially not from prison. I'm doing what's best for SJ and I and I don't care if you like it or not. Despite all the hell you put me through; I was still nice enough to let you be a part of his life so you should be the last person making demands. I guess you forgot about all that huh? So don't sit here and tell me what I better do or today will be the last visit we make."

Shawn Quietly shifted in his seat, sat back, and stared at me for a minute. "I know I was wrong for what I did and I'm doing what I can to make up for it. I can only do but so much in here that's why I'm gonna do everything I can to be there for him when I get out of here." I sighed. "Candy I understand you were put in a bad position and you did what you had to do but I don't want nobody trying to take my place as his father."

"Is that what you're worried about? Shawn no one's gonna take your place. SJ knows who you are and I made sure of that. I never spoke badly about you or tried to hide who you were from him even after everything you did…"

"Well regardless of what you think I do appreciate you bringing SJ up here to see me."

As SJ sat on my lap, I held the phone up to his ear. "Hi Daddy." SJ smiled.

"Hey lil man, Daddy misses you. I'm sorry I missed your birthday. I'm definitely going to make it up to you." Shawn stared at SJ and smiled. After talking a bit more an officer opened up the door behind Shawn and told him it was time to go. Shawn stood up and smiled at me. "Thanks for bringing SJ back to see me."

"No problem, we'll be back to see you in a couple of weeks just take it easy in there."

"I will." We watched Shawn walk off then headed back to the house to meet Taye.

"How'd everything go?"

"It was cool, Shawn was happy to see SJ. He was still harping a little about us staying with you, but he's getting over it."

Taye got quiet for a minute. "I saw your things packed up. You going somewhere?"

"I was gonna tell you I found an apartment." I smiled.

"Candy I don't mind y'all staying here. You don't have to leave if you don't want to."

"Well I figured we'd worn out our welcome. We've been here going on four months now."

Taye took SJ from my arms and held him as I put my purse down to get comfortable. "Candy I don't want y'all to leave. I like having you and SJ around. Besides I don't see no point of staying in this house by myself."

"I don't know Taye. Are you sure about this?"

"Yes." Taye grabbed our suitcases and took them upstairs.

It's now a month later and Taye and I are doing great. We're finally officially dating, but taking it slow so I'm extremely happy and he's wonderful with SJ. Today is Niki and Donte's wedding and I'm excited for them. I'm supposed to be one of Niki's bridesmaids so I've been scrambling around the house all morning trying to get ready. Niki and I became friends after everything that happened with Shawn in court. She said if I had never told her about Shawn messing around on her at his bachelor's party she would've ended up marrying him and been miserable for the rest of her life. Thanks to Shawn I gained a new friend.

"Taye you dressed yet?"

"Yeah just about." Taye came downstairs and grabbed SJ so I could finish getting ready.

"Come on Taye we need to get going."

Chapter 25

Niki

I postponed my wedding for a few weeks to care for Tanya after everything that went down with her. She had a miscarriage from all the stress she endured and had to stay in the hospital for about two weeks. She seems to be doing a little better but she's still not a hundred percent. I couldn't see myself getting married without my sister being there plus Tanya needed me more than ever. Since Darnelle's death, she doesn't speak as much. But she still insisted on helping me with the wedding and refused to let me postpone it any further.

"So today's the big day, how do you feel?" Tanya sat down next to me.

"I'm good, just a little nervous. I'm sure Donte is the one and I'm happy about marrying him. I just can't believe I'm actually getting married."

"Me either you always swore up and down that you'd never get married or have kids now look at you."

Tanya smiled then hugged me. "It seems like everything happened so fast. Just a few months ago we were sitting in

Cynthia's office talking about seating charts, color schemes, and photos. Now here it is our wedding day. It's like someone just pushed the fast forward button or something."

"Yeah I know it did come fast." Tanya looked at me and smiled. "Well sis, we better get going. You don't want to keep the groom waiting." Tanya helped me grab my things then we headed to the hotel where the wedding and reception would be held.

My bridesmaids rushed back and forth across the room grabbing this and that while I was getting my hair and makeup done. Layla stormed in with attitude. "Umm y'all need to hurry up the limo is almost here for the pictures."

I turned around in my seat to face Layla. "The pictures aren't supposed to be taken for another hour and a half."

"Well obviously you haven't looked at the schedule and seeing how you're the bride you should know these things already."

"Layla why are you even here? I specifically told Cynthia I did not want you around for my wedding."

Layla stood in the doorway with her hands on her hips. "Cynthia sent me up here to tell you to hurry up."

"Okay you've said what you had to say so you can leave now."

"I'll leave when I'm ready." Layla smirk and continued to stand in the doorway looking stupid.

"Charlene will you go downstairs and get Cynthia for me? And tell her it's urgent. I'm not finna deal with this shit today." I turned back around in my chair so my stylist could finish my hair and makeup.

A few minutes later Charlene returned with Cynthia. "Is everything okay?" Cynthia rushed through the door as Layla continued to stare.

"No, I want Layla to leave. I don't want her helping out with my wedding today and as far as I'm concerned she's good as fired because I did not pay my money to put up with her mess today."

"Be a woman about yours and speak to me. I'm standing right here. It's not Cynthia you got the problem with it's me so say what you got to say." Layla walked closer to me.

"You know I don't like you Layla and you've known that since day one so don't act brand new. The only reason why you're still around is because of Cynthia, your ass would've been gone if it were up to me."

"Well clearly your man had other plans for me and that's why I'm still here." Layla smirked.

"Please Donte ain't thinking about you or you wouldn't be sitting here watching me get married to him today."

"Well maybe I'll go pay him a visit when I leave your room. I'm sure I can make him happy to see me. I promise you once he gets a taste of this what you think you have won't be an issue anymore."

I was ready to go round to round with this bitch. I balled up my fist and started walking towards her but Tanya pulled me back. "Niki it's your wedding day don't let this hoe get under your skin, she's not worth it."

"Who you calling a hoe?" Layla walked up in Tanya's face, but I jumped in front of her and pushed Layla back.

I tried to warn her and told her, "If you know what's good for you you'd gone about your business."

"Okay and if I don't?" Layla put her finger on my forehead

and pushed it back, so I grabbed her hand and twisted one of her fingers in an attempt to break it off. Wedding or not I refuse to let this heffa come in here and disrespect me the way she had. Layla grabbed my hair with her free hand and pulled me forward so I continued to kick at her until one landed in her stomach. She crouched down in pain so I grabbed her by her hair and yanked her backwards then started to drag her out of the room but Charlene and Tanya stopped me.

"Come on Niki let her go you shouldn't be fighting on your wedding day." Cynthia walked over and started helping Layla to her feet but as soon as she got her balance she tackled me and we both fell to the floor. She tried to pin me down but I took a fist full of her hair and used it as leverage to bang my fist in her face. After a minute of rolling around on the floor, I was finally able to flip her over so I could get on top of her. I grabbed her head and hit it against the floor. I didn't plan to stop until I drew blood. Tanya and a few of the other bridesmaids literally had to pry me off of her.

"You need to go!" Tanya yelled to Layla hoping she'd listen. Layla rolled over on her side and groaned in pain while holding her head.

"That bitch is done. I don't want to see her face again or next time it'll be worse!" Tanya and two of the other bridesmaids dragged me to the bathroom to get me cleaned up. We didn't have much time left for the wedding to start so everyone worked quickly to pull me back together. When I came out of the bathroom and sat down in front of the mirror so my stylist could do my hair and makeup over Layla ran up out of nowhere and pushed me out of my chair then turned to walk out the room. Unwilling to let it go I pulled myself up off the floor then ran up behind her and yanked her back by her dress, causing it to rip. As punches were thrown back and forth, Tanya and Charlene struggled to break it up.

Candy heard the commotion from the hall and stood in the doorway in shock. "What the hell is going on? Are y'all crazy!" Suddenly three cops stormed past Candy and grabbed me and Layla then put us in handcuffs. They escorted us downstairs and put us in the back of two separate squad cars. I looked out the back window slightly disappointed that I let things get this far but I just couldn't let it go. I don't take disrespect very well. Just as we were about to pull off Cynthia, the hotel manager, and some of my wedding party came running out to the cars escorted by two police officers.

The hotel manager pointed at me and said, "You can let her go, I'm not pressing charges."

"What about the other lady?" One of the officers asked.

"You can take her. She caused all this. She was the reason for all the commotion and things getting broken up in my hotel. I will definitely be pressing charges against her." I let out a sigh of relief. Lord knows I didn't want to go to jail today. That would've been one hell of a story for the books. How do I tell people I got locked up for fighting the day of my wedding? Fortunately for me, everyone in the room including Cynthia vouched for me and admitted that Layla started the fight.

The hotel threatened to cancel the wedding fearing that more drama would occur, but I promised them we wouldn't be causing any more problems. I even agreed to give them extra money, on top of the deposit I'd already paid, to take care of any damages we may have caused. Satisfied with my terms the hotel agreed to let me have my wedding so we immediately rushed upstairs to get ready. Somehow my bridal party managed to keep the incident with Layla quiet. All that drama put my wedding almost two hours behind schedule. My wedding party calmed everyone down by claiming that I was running late due to a wardrobe malfunction.

My hair was all over my head, my makeup was smeared, and my bracelet was broken from rolling around on the floor with Layla. So now we're all running around like chickens with our heads cut off trying to hurry up and get ready. An hour and a half later we were all finally ready. Thankfully, my stylist was able to call in some back up to help her out with all of our makeup and hair or we definitely wouldn't have finished this fast.

I finally began making my way down the aisle and I must admit seeing Donte standing at the end of it waiting on me caused my heart to flutter. Doing my best not to shed too many tears I continued to look forward and smiled at what would be my future. Once in front of Donte he pulled my veil over my head and the preacher began the ceremony. I looked around to see Tanya, Charlene, Candy and a few other people crying which almost made me cry as well. Donte took his finger and wiped away one single tear while saying, "I do" to our union. I began to get nervous when the preacher asked if anyone objected to us getting married. It was quiet for a minute and when the preacher started to talk again someone in the crowd yelled, "I do! I object to them getting married."

Everyone looked on as James stood up and walked to the center of the aisle as if he was about to make an announcement. "Niki I just wanted you to know that I understand why you didn't take my proposal and I'm sorry for causing you so much confusion, but I honestly do love you." Donte looked over at me then at James with his fist balled up ready to fight but Mason grabbed his arm to hold him back. James walked towards us and stood at the end of the aisle. "Look man I know you hate me, but I didn't come here to break up y'all wedding I just have a couple things I need to get off my chest." James faced me and I could tell Donte wanted to kill him but Mason stood in front of him to prevent him from catching a charge. "Niki I just want to apologize for making things hard for you. I know you love Donte and I never meant to get in the way of that so I came here to tell you personally that I won't be bothering you anymore and I only want to see you happy. So congratulations and I wish both of you the best of luck." James extended his hand for Donte to shake and as Donte reached out his right hand, he came across with a left hook connecting with James jaw. Caught off guard James fell backwards and hit the floor.

"Now we good." Donte smiled as a couple of the groomsmen escorted James out of the building. After all the commotion died down the preacher continued with the ceremony and we were finally married.

It's a year later and Donte and I are doing great. We've moved into a new home and have been working on having a baby hopefully within the next year. Our wedding and reception was a blast. I explained the details of everything that happened with James to Donte and surprisingly he didn't get mad. He told me he understood why I wanted to handle the situation on my own because he knew that had he done it there wouldn't have been much talking. In all honesty, Donte was satisfied with just knocking him out one good time which his boasts about till this day. I swear

I laugh every time I think about it. As for James, as promised, he never bothered me again so of course I'm happy and thankful for that. Outside of that, everything's been great.

My sister Tanya still hasn't gotten used to being a single parent, but with the help of me and many others she manages to get by and does a great job taking care of Danielle. She often goes by Darnelle's gravesite and sometimes takes Danielle along with her to leave drawings she created in school or to leave flowers and just say hi. She's also going back to school to practice law just like her big sis, which makes me happy. Once she earns her degree Mrs. Conway wants her to run her law firm on the days that she's away. So slowly but surely she's moving on with her life and given a few more years she'll be back to her old self again or at least close to it.

Chapter 26

Candy

After a bit of persuasion from Taye along with an incident that occurred at the grocery store I finally decided to stop stripping and take classes to become an RN. One day while I was with SJ in the grocery store I noticed a man staring at me. While standing in the checkout line the man approached me. "Excuse me didn't you work at that strip club in St. Louis called Fantasy back in the day?"

"No, I think you got me mixed up with somebody else." Embarrassed and noticing all eyes were on me I prayed that the line would move a little quicker.

"Nah, I'm sure it was you. You're that stripper umm…" The man snapped his fingers while trying to jog his memory. "Candy! That's your name!"

"Hell everybody be requesting you for bachelor parties. Yeah, I saw you strip one night. You sure know how to do some things with a pole." The man eyeballed me from head to toe as he grinned from ear to ear.

"Look mister gone about your business." I told him

through gritted teeth as I rushed to pay for my groceries.

The man followed me to the parking lot and asked, "You still do parties? I'd love to have you strip for my boy's birthday. I heard you do favors and everything so how much do you charge for that? We got the money just name your price."

"Look, I don't strip anymore so leave me the fuck alone!"

"Damn you ain't got to be like that sweetheart. I just thought you might want some extra business." The man backed up with his has in the air as if he surrendered.

"Nah I'm good." I felt cheap and embarrassed as I watched the man stroll off. I decided at that very moment that I'd never strip again. That turned out to be a great decision that came with many perks. Niki was ecstatic and began sending me money regularly to help out with SJ and pay for school. Even Shawn was proud of me for quitting and he sent every dime he earned in prison for selling cigarettes or whatever else to take care of SJ. Unfortunately, Shawn won't be getting out anytime soon but he still remains hopeful. Recently he went to a parole hearing and based off of good behavior his sentence was reduced from seven years to five meaning he only has about two more years to serve, so things are beginning to look up for him.

Taye finally announced to his Aunt Gloria that we were officially a couple. I guess he was waiting for me to change my lifestyle before making things with me official, which I could understand. What man likes knowing everybody had seen and sampled what he has? I guess it's not a good look. Anyway, I feel much better about myself and I no longer mind telling people what I do for a living. For the first time in my life, I'm actually happy. As for my cousin Tia, she finally found proof that Thomas was cheating when she caught him with another woman in her bed. Tia kicked their asses all over that room then threw him and the woman out with no clothes on. The woman hopped in her car and peeled off while Thomas pathetically beat on the door butt naked in broad daylight begging to be let back in. Tia packed all of his clothes in a suitcase and kindly sat them outside for him to retrieve then had a locksmith to come out the same day and change the locks on all the doors. Since then she has spent every day trying to make things right between us, but unfortunately I'm not ready to forgive and forget. Maybe one day in the distant future that'll change, but as for right now, it's not happening.

Chapter 27

Mason

Ariel continued to try her hand with Charlene and I until I filed claims against her for being an unfit mother. Faced with losing Nate, she talked me into dropping the charges and agreed to stay away from us for good but not without warning that all bets are off if the agreement is broken.

Not having to deal with Ariel anymore was a blessing for Charlene and I. Charlene was no longer angry and stressed out and she delivered two healthy twin babies, one boy and one girl with no complications. How great is that! I am thrilled about being a first time father and finally able to enjoy my life and my family.

After much thought I decided to make Charlene a permanent fixture in my life legally, so during her birthday party in front of all our family and friends I got down on one knee and proposed to her. I barely got to get the words out my mouth before she said yes and snatched the ring out my hand causing everyone to laugh. I smiled as I watched her go around the room showing off her ring to all her friends. I knew with all my heart this was the right decision and couldn't wait till the day that I could call her my wife, which we planned for the following year.

Also in Stores

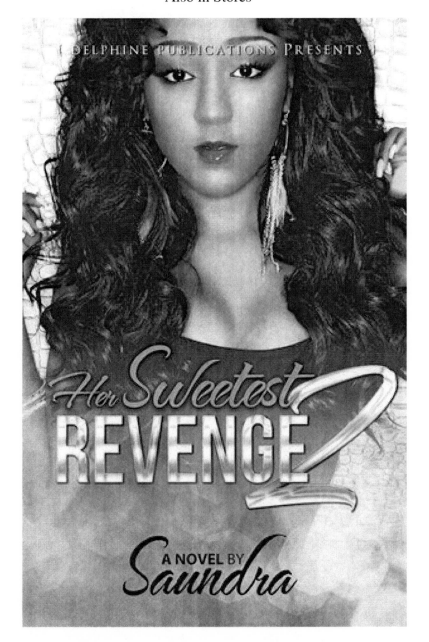

DELPHINE PUBLICATIONS PRESENTS

Her Sweetest REVENGE 2

A NOVEL BY Saundra

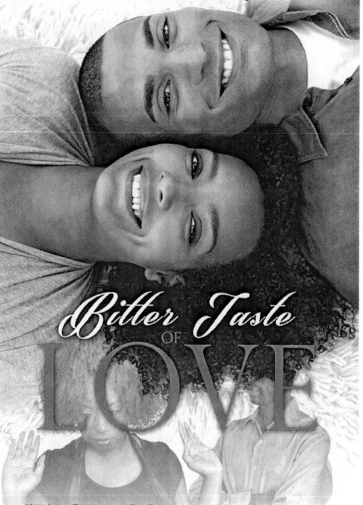

(DELPHINE PUBLICATIONS Presents)

Bitter Taste
OF
LOVE

STACEY COVINGTON-LEE

AUTHOR OF *THE KNIFE IN MY BACK*

THE
Ultimate
No 4 No

TAMIKA NEWHOUSE

AUTHOR OF *KISSES DON'T LIE*

WE ARE TEAM DELPHINE

Follow us on Twiter and Instargram
@DeplphinePub
FB: DelphinePublicatons
www.DelphinePublications.com

4/14: 1/23/14

CPSIA information can be obtained at www.ICGtesting.com
Printed in the USA
LVOW13s0912161013

357172LV00001B/121/P

9 780989 090636